Caribbean

The CANZUK at War Series

Book 0.5

Dedication:

To my old man, Bob Flannagan:
A steady presence. A man who encourages through his interest, his actions, and kindness.

Author's Note: CANZUK is an alliance comprised of Canada, Australia, New Zealand and the United Kingdom. Caribbean Payback is a standalone novella in the larger CANZUK at War universe.

Chapter 1

Haiti, Port-au-Prince

Not for the first time, she marveled at the drabness of this cursed city. Everywhere Captain Veronique Bertrand looked were the ramshackle, grey concrete-block homes that made up the vast majority of the buildings in Port-au-Prince. The roofs of the tightly-packed structures didn't help. It was the dull grey of sun-tired tin or the red rust of sheet metal that had long given into the unforgiving heat and rain of the Caribbean.

And the smell. She would never get used to the combination of rotting garbage and fresh shit. With the exception of the city's few affluent neighborhoods, the stench was ubiquitous and clung to you like some desperate drunk at one of the nightclubs she would visit on her occasional trip to Montreal. She looked forward to the day she was out of this hapless country so the ripe stink would no longer infect her nostrils.

The ride from United Nations Square to their destination in that part of the capital called Martissant shouldn't have taken more than twenty minutes, but they were coming up on twice that. The lag in their schedule didn't concern her anywhere near as much as the absence of people out and about this morning.

As they approached the dirt patch of a soccer pitch where she and a platoon from the Royal 22nd Regiment, or the Vandoos, as they were called in Canada, would work with a local non-governmental organization to set up one of the UN's too-infrequent food distribution and medical stations, Bertrand took in a loose gaggle of desperate-looking Haitians. In her five months in-country, she had lost count of how many times they had visited this same location to oversee and provide security for the NGO's outreach program. In each previous instance, she had found hundreds of people already waiting at the pitch where the clinic would distribute its medicines and nutrition as long as its supplies lasted.

As she watched the first of the convoy's up-armored Mercedes G-Wagons take a right off Route des Dalles into a small copse of trees that would lead them to the dirt-brown playing field, she grabbed the radio handset from the dash of her vehicle. "All vehicles, this is Shepherd Actual. Shepherd Two and Three, I need you to slow up on your approach to the distribution area and take a good look around. Everyone else, come to a halt. Am I the only one who's noticed that there aren't a lot of the locals around? Did we miss the memo – is today a national holiday?"

"Or these people are too fucking lazy or high to drag themselves out from whatever holes they live in to come and get the help they need," said the ever-bitter Master Corporal driving Bertrand's G-Wagon.

She had long ago stopped her efforts to soften the man's attitude. From the hinterlands of Quebec, Soulier, was by far her unit's harshest critic of the locals. But for all his insensitive commentary, when it came to getting the work done, the man performed as well as any other soldier in the outfit. The Canadian Armed Forces or the CAF as it was known by those in the military had spent years and millions in an effort to better shape the hearts and minds of its soldiers. In Soulier's case, the effort hadn't stuck. She would again note the behavior in her mission debrief so it could be more thoroughly followed up on when they were back home.

Making sure her radio handset in her hand was un-toggled, Bertrand snapped at her driver, "Check that shit, Soulier. If you can't empathize with the locals that's fine, but for my sake and that of my career, do me a favor and keep your mouth shut while I'm on the horn."

"Copy that, Captain. Will save the unwelcome commentary for when you're not addressing the troops," the soldier said with what Bertrand recognized was a faux smile.

She ignored him. There would be time enough to deal with him when they were back home.

Her attention reverted to their ongoing mission as she heard her radio burp in response to her earlier question. "Shepherd Actual, this is Shepherd Two. Copy your order. Shepherd Three and I will roll up, and let you know what there is to see. We've noted the absence of the locals too. Could be that the NGO didn't do a great job of advertising today's clinic. It's happened before."

"Copy that, Shepherd Two," said Bertrand. "In the meantime, I'll put in for drone support from HQ. We're the only ones on the road as far as I know, so they should be able to have something up ASAP. Something isn't right this morning. I can feel it. Let me know what you see once you get on the field. We'll keep the engines ready and if we need to, we'll ride up on you looking badass."

"Copy that, Actual, we're moving onto the soccer field as I speak. Everything looks on the up-and-up. There's a pair of trucks from Life for Relief and a couple of dozen locals standing around. It's fewer than we're used to seeing but other than that, it looks okay."

"What about the treeline on the right and the compound on the northeast end of the field?" asked Bertrand. "If I was going to take a run at us, that's where I'd be."

The radio paused momentarily. "Ahh... looks good from here, boss. Wait... hold up. We've got movement in the treeline. Males. They're dressed like locals. Wait... Jesus fuck, they're armed! We've got incoming!"

Two hundred meters away, Bertrand heard the distinct crack of dozens of automatic weapons open up. Over the small arms fire, she heard Shepherd Two yell across the radio, "Contact, contact, contact! We've got multiple hostiles in the treeline and we've got what looks like a machine gun crew setting up on the roof of the compound. They'll have us in a crossfire within the minute. We have multiple civilians who are down. We're taking heavy fire, boss, permission to return fire."

Bertrand didn't hesitate. The too-strict rules of engagement for the UN mission could go to hell. "Permission granted, Shepherd Two. Open up with everything you've got. I'll be on your position in moments. Hold tight. Actual out."

Forcing her voice to remain deliberate and calm, she addressed the rest of the security detail. "Task Force Shepherd, we are getting out of here. Shepherd Seven, Eight, Nine - you are to lead the logistics team to Rendezvous Point Lima. You are not to stop for anything. Shepherd Seven, you have point. Move out now."

"Copy that, Actual. We're moving now. Shepherd Seven out."

As Bertrand heard a loud boom emanate from the direction of the soccer field, three G-Wagons quickly rolled past her. Atop each of the armored four-by-fours, a soldier manned a pintled-mounted machine gun and each was carefully scanning their section of the road. As they began to pick up speed, several of the convoy's logistics vehicles followed them, each truck accelerating to bring themselves into the right position relative to the vehicle in front of them. Everyone under her command knew the drill and knew it well.

As she listened to the crackle of gunfire, her eye caught movement down the road. Right at a slight bend in the thoroughfare, a pair of large, rough-looking trucks came together nose to nose at the center of their westbound route. "Tabernac," Bertrand cursed.

On the back of each truck, men began to pop into view. Each was toting a weapon of some kind. As the G-Wagon that was Shepherd Seven slowed down to face off with the new threat, she heard several sharp cracks to her immediate left.

Driven by the instinct of self-preservation, her eyes lanced in the direction of the new threat. In between the buildings on the other side of the road and on several rooftops, she could see armed men firing in the direction of the G-Wagons that had remained with her.

The vehicle's radio handset still in her hand, Bertrand brought the unit to her mouth and called out, "Ambush, ambush, ambush! All units, all units, you have permission to fire on any hostile holding a weapon. Have an eye for legit civilians. All remaining units are to advance..."

Before she had the opportunity to finish giving her orders, the driver-side window of her vehicle exploded inwards showering her with chunks of glass. She heard a loud grunt and felt something wet spray across her face. In that moment, Soulier was pressed up against her, his left hand at his neck, while his right hand still gripped the steering wheel. In the rear seat, she could hear the welcome chug of the turreted C-6 machine gun issuing rhythmic five-round bursts.

Placing the handset back to her mouth, "All units, all units - advance toward Shepherd Seven's position. We will consolidate around his position and fight past the ambush point on Route des Dalles, making our way to RV Lima. Get moving, everyone. That includes you, too, Shepherd Two and Three. Blanchet and Dube, get the hell out of there, now!"

Bertrand counted to three and said again, "Shepherd Two and Three, do you copy?"

As she felt her own G-Wagon begin to move, her eyes moved to Soulier. He said nothing as he looked forward intently and drove. His left hand, covered in blood, was pressed against the side of his neck. He looked terribly pale.

A new voice burst onto the radio. "Shepherd Actual, this is Gator Four, what is your status? Is that gunfire coming from your position? Gator Actual is requesting a sitrep and advises that if any of your units are firing their weapons, they are to cease fire immediately. I repeat, any units firing their weapons are to cease fire immediately."

"Gator Four, this is Shepherd Actual, that is a negative on the cease-fire. We were ambushed and fired upon by a well-armed force and we have wounded and potentially several KIAs. We are taking fire from multiple directions, and I've given the order for a fighting retreat. I'm requesting eyes in the sky and reinforcements from the rapid reaction force to our location. We're just west of the soccer field on Route des Dalles. Advise. Shepherd Actual out."

To the rear, Bertrand heard a yelp and turned in time to see the knees of her topside machine gunner buckle. The man, one Corporal Rivet, had slid from the turret and was now slumped across the back seat moaning in pain. A portion of his jaw was missing and as a result, his face was now a horror show of blood and exposed bone.

A too-calm, Irish-accented male voice came onto the radio speaking English. "Shepherd Actual, this is Gator Actual, what is your status? May I remind you that our rules of engagement dictate that we are to use minimum force and only in response to an active threat. I hear lots of automatic gunfire coming from your direction, Shepherd. It sounds like a bloody warzone out there. What the hell is going on?"

Bertrand ignored the voice and took in the scene now in front of her. The front end of one of her four logistic trucks had begun to burn. The remaining three were arrayed behind their three G-Wagon escorts, of which only two were exchanging fire with men on the back of the trucks that had blocked their escape route. Other soldiers from the convoy, men from the security force and several of the logistics soldiers, were behind engine blocks or some other type of cover and were returning fire with their own personal weapons.

Bertrand counted three bodies on the ground and saw the convoy's medics working feverishly on another soldier on the pavement behind the logistics truck immediately in front of her.

As Soulier brought their vehicle to a sharp stop behind the loaded flatbed stacked high with food and medical supplies, she turned to the wounded man and said, "Grab Rivet, and get to the medics."

Somehow, the man had got his hands on a tourniquet. The bandage was soaked with fresh red blood, but despite this, he gave her a glare and said, "I'm good. I can still drive."

"Bullshit. Get Rivet and get the fuck out of here now!" Bertrand barked. "I'll grab somebody else. I haven't heard from Blanchet and

Dube. I've got to go back to the soccer field to see what's up. You're no good to me the way you are now. Move, Master Corporal. Now!" She nearly screamed the final word.

The wounded soldier gave her one last hard look and then opened the door. In seconds, he had grabbed Rivet from the backseat and together they shambled toward the harried medics.

She took up the vehicle's handset. "Gator Actual, this is Shepherd Actual. Do you copy?"

"We copy you, Shepherd. I need your status report, Captain," said the Irishman.

"We continue to engage an enemy force that is of company strength – at least. We were ambushed at RV Bravo and continue to be under heavy fire. They have automatic and high-caliber weapons. I have multiple dead and wounded. We're going to consolidate at my current position, then we're going to put down smoke and make a break for it. We continue to return fire. I repeat, I have not ordered a ceasefire. Have the rapid reaction force waiting for us at RV Lima. I'll issue a sitrep in five. Shepherd Actual out."

"Shepherd Actual, that's unacceptable. I'm giving you a direct order to ceasefire. You need to de-escalate the situation. You have to try and start a dialogue with them. This has to be some kind of mistake."

Bertrand's hand reached out and savagely turned off the radio, and said, "Fucking Irish prick." Grabbing her C-8 carbine, she opened her door and walked in the direction of the small triage area in front of her G-Wagon.

Excluding her own vehicle, her platoon's remaining G-Wagons had encircled their position, and soldiers were now in each vehicles' turrets, lashing out steady bursts of machine-gun fire at the two trucks blocking their way and in the direction of the ambushers now behind them. It wasn't an ideal situation, but for the moment, they had a standoff. As she stood in the shadow of the rearmost logistics truck and did her best to filter out the sounds of moaning soldiers and automatic weapons fire, her eyes found the person she was looking for.

"Vincent," she yelled to a squat man twenty meters away standing behind the engine block of one of the up-armored SUVs. Hearing his name, the commander of the platoon that had drawn responsibility for the security element of the morning's mission immediately locked eyes with her, smiled, and without a moment's hesitation, left his position and with his body bent, hustled toward her.

Arriving, the lieutenant said, "What a shitshow, Vee."

"That's one word for it. Listen, it looks like we're on our own for the next fifteen at least. O'Regan wants us to stand down if you can believe it?"

"Stand down? You told him to fuck off, I hope."

"I didn't get the chance. I lost radio contact. Or that's gonna be the story when we make it back. Listen, if I take two of the Wagons, do you think you can hold these bastards off until the reaction force arrives."

"We can hold. We can make our ammo last and as long as we have the C-6s going, they won't come at us. They're not that stupid or brave by the looks of it. You gonna head back to the soccer field?"

"Yeah. It's been radio silence from them since this thing kicked off," said Bertrand.

"Don't worry," the thickly built younger man said. Incredibly, he was still sporting his signature smile. "Blanchet and Dube know their business. They're two of my best guys, eh."

"Yeah, well, there's no way I'm waiting here while they have all the fun. Hold the fort, Lieutenant. If I know the colonel, he'll already have the RRF rolling, regardless of what the Irishman says."

"No doubt about that, Captain. Fucking wild horses couldn't stop Michaud from getting here. The only question is how soon."

Vincent held out his fist and Bertrand quickly fist-bumped it and said, "I'll be back in five with the boys."

"Copy that, Vee. Stay safe."

UN Headquarters, Port-au-Prince

Brigadier General Micheal O'Regan's face was tinged with red and verging in the direction of ugly. The commanding officer of the UN's latest mission in Haiti was beyond displeased with the current situation.

"Lt. Colonel Michaud, your Captain Bertrand is in a whole hell of a lot of trouble. Need I remind you of what happened the last time a civilian got killed by one of your trigger-happy soldiers? I thought Canadians were professionals who took pride in their role as peacekeepers, but I see you're nothing more than a bunch of shoot-first-ask-questions-later cowboys. No doubt the Americans would be right proud of the mess that you're making, but as you well know, the Americans aren't a part of this mission and thank goodness for that. Your captain is playing right into the hands of the gangs, and I'll have no part of it."

Michaud stared back at the man, doing a masterful job of keeping the fury he felt from poisoning the look on his face. "Sir, my soldiers – soldiers under your command – are under fire, and by the sounds of it, some of them are wounded or maybe dead. Are you going to order in the Rapid Reaction Force or not?"

"How can I order in the RRF, if I don't know what's going on? You've heard the captain, or more accurately, you've heard very little from her. I asked for details, and she blew me off. How do you expect me to risk throwing more fuel on the fire without having more information? Tell me, Colonel, what do they not teach Canadian infantry officers about situational reporting and following the chain of command?"

Michaud placed his hands on his hips. Despite the madness that was Haiti, he still believed in the work they were doing. But he was no warrior-diplomat and the Canadian generals who had signed off on his current role knew that. In fact, he had been told explicitly that he'd been given this command because the Canadian military knew that O'Regan was foremost a bureaucrat-soldier who was more keen on his next career move than he was on commanding soldiers. Whether she had known it or not, Michaud thought, in prioritizing her soldiers' welfare over UN force commander's need to control the situation, Veronique Bertrand had given this sandbagger of an officer the cover he needed to dodge the fall out of what was to come.

"Sir, I've already ordered up one of our drones to recce the situation. I thought you should know that," said Michaud.

"Of course you have, Colonel. And no doubt you're going to tell me that you'll be taking the Canadian element of the RRF and heading to Bertrand's position whether or not I order the RRF to dispatch."

"That's correct, sir," Michaud said evenly. "I would add that not having heard back from Captain Bertrand suggests there is a comms issue at play. Perhaps she's being jammed. Perhaps her radio has been disabled. If she can't communicate with us, the only way we're going to get more intel on what's happening is to get there ourselves and see what's going on."

"Save it, Colonel Michaud. You can write up excuses in your after-action report once this disaster your people have created is cleaned up," said O'Regan dismissively.

"I'll do that, sir," Michaud replied and, without saluting, turned his back on the other man and made his way to the door of the mission's command center.

As he reached the doorway, he heard O'Regan call to him. "I warned against allowing Canada to make up the security element of this mission. Somewhere in the past thirty years, your country lost its way. Go be the hero, Colonel. It's what you wannabe Americans do now, isn't it? Well, this mission will have no part of it. As you walk out that door, know that you're doing so against my direct order."

Five minutes later and in full battle kit, Michaud rode in the third vehicle of a fast-moving convoy. He was in one of four Canadian G-

Wagons following a pair of behemoth Romanian Piranha V Infantry Fighting Vehicles, IFVs.

After a full decade of Canadian fighter jets helping to train Romanian pilots and patrolling that country's airspace as a part of NATO, the major in charge of the Romanian contingent attached to the RRF had not hesitated in answering Michaud's personal plea for assistance.

When Michaud had tried to explain the extraordinary nature of his request, the Romanian officer only flipped his hand in an uncaring fashion and had said, "You don't need to explain. In fact, the less I know the better. That Irish bastard has not told me I can't go, so I will make my own decision."

After a moment's hesitation, the Romanian officer said in his thickly accented voice, "What's the word in English when you figure out your own way?"

"Discretion?" offered Michaud.

"Yes, yes, that's the one. I will use my own discretion and if things go poorly for us, I know what my country's generals will say. 'You had our ally's back. You did good.' End of discussion."

His G-Wagon's radio flared to life, tearing him away from his recollection of the recent interaction with the Romanian officer. "Bandit Actual, this is Falcon Three, we have a visual on the soccer field. It should be on your tac pad now."

As his driver expertly worked to avoid the horrendous potholes smeared across the surface of the road they were sprinting along, Michaud took in the high-def image of four vehicles near the centre of a brown playing field. He could see that one of the four had caught on fire, with thick black smoke billowing out from the G-Wagon's engine block.

Perhaps two dozen meters east of the vehicles, seven soldiers wearing Canadian army uniforms were lined up on their knees. To their front were perhaps two dozen men, all of them armed. Whoever these thugs were, they were wearing a riot of clothing that differed in all aspects with the exception that each man was wearing a black balaclava to cover his face. He watched in growing concern as several of the armed men walked forward in the direction of his soldiers, their weapons at the ready.

"Falcon Three, tighten your visual on our boys," Michaud said urgently.

"Copy that Actual," the operator said.

As the drone's camera adjusted its image, he toggled the frequency on his radio. "Bandit Four, this is Bandit Actual. I need you to pick up the pace up front. We need to get to that soccer field ASAP. Drive her like you stole her, Darius."

The voice of the Romanian major responded immediately. "Copy that. Traffic's light this morning and we Romanians can drive as fast as the next Euro, so hold onto something tight Actual. Bandit Four out."

The Football Pitch, Port-au-Prince

"What do we have here? Oh, look at you, sweetheart. Aren't you a pretty thing? Isn't she pretty, boys? Look at those eyes. Blue. We don't see those around here often, do we? And an officer, no less. Today is our day!" The pudgy man who was speaking reached out with his hand and grabbed her chin, tilting Bertrand's face upward.

On her knees at the far left of the kneeling line of her soldiers, she stared back defiantly at the man who had a surprising vice-like grip on her jaw. While most of the gang's faces were covered by balaclavas, this man's was not and he was an ugly thing. His eyes were bloodshot, his face was round like a taut beachball, and when he offered her his leering smile, a collection of misaligned and yellowed teeth was put on display.

"Reinforcements are on their way. Leave us, get out of here now, and no more of your men have to die. There's been enough death today already," Bertrand said, injecting as much authority as she could into her words.

"Ah, my sweet thing. Telling me how it's going to be, are you? You arrogant bitch. Just like your country."

Faster than Bertrand would have thought possible, the open palm of the man's hand cocked and slapped her across the face, wrenching her jaw and sending a flash of stars across her vision. As pain lanced through her, she poured what remained of her concentration into the task of staying upright on her knees.

As she stabilized herself and refocused her eyes, she heard one of her men to her right bellow a string of threats.

In a quick motion, the man who had slapped her pulled a pistol from his waist, pointed it at the soldier and shot him point-blank in the face. The soldier, Sergeant Dube – a good man with three boys – fell forward face down, his blood quickly saturating the brown dirt underneath his unmoving body.

As other soldiers in the line began to unload with their own curses and threats, Dube's executioner ignored them and took a step back to Bertrand. For a brief moment, their eyes locked and as they did so, his lips peeled back to once again show off his carny-like smile. His eyes then shifted upwards and looked into the sky. Pointing, he said loudly, "Perfect, we have an audience. Let's give them a show, boys!"

In a quick motion, he grabbed her arm and savagely pulled her to her feet. Spinning her around, he grabbed the hair at the back of her head and forced her to look into the cloudless blue sky.

"Do you see it?" he asked.

She could see a small speck in the air. If she had to guess, the tactical drone was at an altitude of two thousand feet. More than close enough for the drone's military-grade camera to see the whites of her eyes.

"Let's give them a show, shall we? A show you and the rest of the world won't soon forget," the man said in a low voice behind her.

Bertrand's head jerked as the man began to pull her in the direction of the men who were faced off against her soldiers. Reaching the center of the armed gaggle, the man spun her around to face her men and then viciously kicked into the back of her legs. She winced as her knees struck the packed ground six meters in front of Dube's body.

"My fellows, it's time to send a message. It is we, Alpha-7, who run this country. Not that double-crossing bitch who claims to be our president, not the UN, and certainly not the country that these neo-colonialists are from," he said loudly while waving his hand in the direction of the remaining soldiers from Bertrand's security detail.

"Canada," the man scoffed. "You're a fucking joke. A country run by a bunch of American wannabes. Pussies, who let their women fight."

The gangster took a knee and placed his face beside Bertrand's. She could smell the man's decaying breath as he issued a heavy sigh. Conversationally, he said, "You will be coming with me. Your men, however. They will stay here."

Raising his voice, he said, "Kill them."

Enroute UN Rapid Reaction Force, Port-au-Prince

In high definition, Michaud watched helplessly as five of his soldiers were gunned down in cold blood. He watched in anger as the maskless thug leveled Bertrand with a blow to the side of her face as she struggled to get to her men. Seconds later, he watched a pair of men drag his now inert junior officer into the copse of trees into which Bertrand, the maskless man, and the rest of the morning's ambushers disappeared, the drone's cameras quickly losing them in the sprawl that was Port-au-Prince.

In all of what Michaud had just seen, a line had been crossed. Canada did not have the martial capacity of the Americans or even her former colonial master, Great Britain. But she wasn't entirely without teeth. With the United States seemingly on a path to a nasty national divorce, recent Canadian governments had made investments in the armed forces that would allow Canada to affect its foreign policy independent of the ongoing shit-show taking place south of the 49th parallel. And if there was one good thing about the unfolding crisis, it was that Haiti was in Canada's geographic neck of the woods. In fact, quite a bit of CAF muscle could be brought to bear on this part of the world, but only if the political leadership of the country had the guts to take action.

Michaud knew very little of politics. He was foremost a fighting man, but what he did know of Canada's current prime minister gave him hope. In her time as PM, she had demonstrated herself to be a wholly more serious person than her predecessor and with an election in the offing, perhaps the table had been set for something serious to be done.

Because even for Canada - passive and diplomatic to a fault - what had just happened would be seen as too much. Of that, Michaud was certain. Someone, somewhere in this God-forsaken country had made a serious miscalculation as to how Canada would react to the death of its soldiers. And now his country was going to make them pay.

Chapter 2

Port-au-Prince

Samuel Petit was supposed to have this week off. He had made plans to spend the day collecting supplies for a long-planned trip to Massif De La Selle, the mountain range in the southeast, where he would summit the highest elevation in Haiti, the spectacular Pic La Selle. But as of nine this morning, his plans of leisure had changed. And dramatically so.

He had received a text on his phone directing him to sign into his account where he had been instructed to find out all that he could about the Alpha-7 gang and the role it had played in the twenty-minute gun battle that most of the city had heard play out only a few hours earlier.

The brief sent to him from his supervisor in the Canadian Security Intelligence Service – CSIS – had been scanty on details, but the gist of it was that eleven Canadian soldiers had been killed as a result of a well-planned ambush and that an officer had been taken away from the mess alive.

On short notice, his contact in the Haitian government had agreed to meet him at Du Cacique Villa Hotel. Strolling into the hotel's poolside lounge, Petit saw his contact immediately and moved to sit in the utilitarian steel chair waiting for him. The other man looked like the bureaucrat that he was. Spindly, spectacled, and sporting the thin mustache in vogue with Haiti's intellectual class, the man had somehow managed to coax whatever comfort he could out of the Spartan-looking chair he was now slouched in. Other than one disinterested-looking member of the wait staff, no one else had taken up residency in the hotel's lounge.

"Jerome, good to see you. Thanks so much for agreeing to meet on short notice," Petit said in Haitian-accented French. "I hope it isn't too much trouble for us to meet like this?"

"It's not a problem. This morning's unfortunate incident has set the city on fire politically, so anyone who might be interested in my extra-curricular activities is most certainly caught up with something else. I take it, it's that same incident you'd like to discuss?"

"It is. Rumor has it that Alpha-7 was involved?" Petit said, as he claimed his own uncomfortable seat.

"Scum, my friend," the bureaucrat replied in feigned concern. "The very worst this city has to offer. As you can understand, details are still unclear, but I've also heard that it was the Sevens that were involved."

Out of the corner of his eye, Petit saw the lounge's only waitress approach their table. Upon reaching them, the slender, plain-looking woman placed a glistening pitcher of water on their table along with a pair of glasses, each with a wedge of lemon perched along their rims. "Would you like something to drink or eat, gentlemen?"

The bureaucrat spoke. "Not at the moment, my sweet. Right now, my friend and I need only a bit of privacy. But don't go too far. I suspect we'll need you later."

The waitress gave the man a weak smile but said nothing. She turned and as she walked away, the oily man sitting across from Petit eyed the woman's retreating form hungrily.

Before the simmering disgust inside him could be allowed to froth, Petit re-claimed the man's attention. "So, what can you tell me about the Sevens? You said you might have valuable information. Certainly, my time is valuable and for today at least, I don't have as much time as I would like."

Hearing Petite's words, the informant trained his eyes on the CSIS officer but said nothing. Though relatively new to the foreign intelligence game, Petite knew straight away what the next step in this dance was.

Though it galled him, he forced a smile onto his lips. What was about to happen made him feel dirty – and more so because he was dealing with the lecherous piece of garbage sitting across from him. But he did know the game and he could play it well. Filling in the silence, Petit said, "Your sister in Montreal has received a payment three times what she normally receives. And if the information you provide is validated, I will ensure a similar payment follows. I'm all ears, my friend."

On hearing of Petit's payment and the chance to earn more cash, a smile bloomed on the bureaucrat's face.

"I will tell you all that I can. I'm sickened to my core by what happened today. In these dark times, it is more important than ever that people such as ourselves help one another, is it not?"

As the man delivered his question, Petit resisted the temptation to reach across the table and belt the self-serving man across the face. But as satisfying as that might be, he was a professional and so he only reciprocated the slick bureaucrat's smile with his own and said, "You help me, I help you. We both continue to win, Jerome. Now tell me all you can about the Alpha-7s and this Emanuel Jean fellow."

————

Montreal

The sound of a driver making solid contact with a golf ball filled the air. A man close by whistled.

"Beauty drive, Lenny. Right down the middle. What's that – about 285? Looks like you've finally figured out that driver."

Lenny Baptiste canted his upper body and gracefully pulled his tee from the ground. "Bout time, Jimmy. God knows I paid enough for this thing."

Walking off the first tee of the Islemere Golf Course in Montreal, Baptiste spied two men in Canadian army fatigues walking in his direction from the club house. "Interesting," Baptiste said aloud.

Catching that something had caught their stout friend's attention, the rest of the foursome stopped what they were doing and as a group, they took in the two men purposely striding toward them in the distance.

Remi Henri, a successful car salesman and a long-time friend who had served in the Royal Canadian Regiment with Baptiste ages before, crossed his arms over his chest and said, "They don't look happy. And it looks like they've locked on to you, Lenny. What did you do? I thought you were retired?"

"I am," said Baptiste quickly. "For ten months and my old lady has never been happier."

As the two soldiers arrived at their location, the taller of the two men said, "Warrant Officer Baptiste?"

"Retired Warrant Officer, Captain," Baptiste corrected the man. "How can I help you on this most wonderful of days?"

"Sorry to intrude, Warrant, but we couldn't get you on your cell."

"Damn right you couldn't because I gave up that thing six months ago and it's the best goddamned thing I ever did."

"Your wife told us as much and let us know we could find you here."

"Whoa, hangfire, son – you called my wife? And she told you I was here? How pissed did she sound on the phone?"

"She was most pleasant with us, sir," said the army captain.

One of the other golfers whistled and said, "Oh man, she's beyond pissed, Lenny. Whatever you did, my man, it's not these two guys you need to worry about. Jenelle is gonna have your ass!"

"Jesus on the GD cross," Baptiste said. "Alright, what the hell do you two want? I turned in all my kit on my last day. Is there some paperwork I missed?"

If the captain found the question funny, he didn't let on. "Sir, folks out of SOFCOM need to speak with you on an urgent matter. We'd like you to come with us."

Baptiste's reply was immediate and perhaps a bit more stern than he had intended. "Son, I think you may have missed the point about me being retired. With respect, I'm not going anywhere."

The captain pulled an oversized smartphone out of his pocket, walked toward Baptiste, and handed him the unit. "Read and watch this, Warrant."

Taking the device, Baptiste began to manipulate the screen, and after a long moment of reading and watching a short video, he handed the smartphone back to the soldier with a grim look on his face.

He turned to his three friends, each of whom was now sporting looks that were some combination of curious and concerned.

"Is everything okay, Lenny?" asked the car salesman. It looks like you've seen a ghost. That or you're about to kill somebody."

"All is good Remi. You guys head out. Something's come up with work."

"Work? Man, you just said you're retired." The words that came from his closest mate held more than a touch of outrage. On Baptiste's retirement from the CAF, the two men's long standing friendship had benefited considerably. They hadn't known each other in Haiti, but the combination of their birth country and their time in the army had forged a bond that had endured the years.

"Retired from reg force, yes, but I put in with the local reserve unit here in town. I was supposed to report in with them next week. Looks like there's some shit going on down south. You know how it goes. They're just looking for a bit of homegrown intel. I'm sure that's all."

"Yeah, I know how it goes my man, and I know whatever it is these two jokers are selling isn't in the interest of a man who's put in his time. You want my advice, brother? Let someone else handle whatever shit is going down. You're not the only Haitian in the goddamned army - of that, I'm certain."

Baptiste looked back at his friend with a resigned look. "It's who I am. Since I was eighteen, the CAF is all I've ever known. If someone thinks I can help... I mean, what harm could come from a bit of consulting work?"

"Yeah, well just make sure consulting is all they get you to do. You owe these guys nothing. You hear me, Lenny. Nothing!" As the other Haitian ex-pat said the words his hand slashed angrily in the direction of the two soldiers.

Baptiste smiled and took heart from his friend's concern. He loved Remi like family. The man had left the army years ago and when he was in it, it had only ever been a job. Then and now, Baptiste had a different connection with the military. It had been his life's work and so he would let his day be interrupted, if grudgingly. "I got you my friend. Consulting only. Now, stop being a little bitch, and hit your ball. I'll see you guys in a couple of days, same place, same time."

"That had better be the case my friend, or else."

"Copy that Remi. Copy that."

——

Ottawa

"The PM has seen the video and she wants a kinetic option drawn up while she and Global Affairs give the diplomatic option the old college try. I was on a call with her twenty minutes ago and I can tell you she is one unhappy lady. On the status of Captain Bertrand, her words were, and I quote, 'They give her up in less than twenty-four hours or we take her back with force, and fuck the consequences. The UN can go to hell for all I care.'"

Canada's Chief of Defence Staff, CDS locked eyes with Major General Nathan Hermes, the officer in charge of Canadian Special Operations Forces Command, CANSOFCOM. "And yes, in case you're wondering, she most certainly did drop an F-bomb. I've never seen her this pissed. She wants Bertrand back, come hell or high water. Seeing that's the direction we're taking, what do you have for me, Nate?"

Hermes was immediate in his reply. "Because we'll need to be quick and dirty, we're aiming to keep things simple. JTF-2 Assault Group A is ready to go. By six this afternoon, they'll be on their way to Port-au-Prince and they'll be wheels down just after dark sets in. They'll be flying in on a pair of CC-150s. We won't be advising the UN of their arrival or anyone else for that matter."

"So we're going to keep O'Regan out of it?" asked the CDS.

"The Irishman will be kept in the dark as long as possible, as will the rest of the mission's senior people. The exception will be the Romanians. Between our own contacts in the Romanian special forces and Global Affairs, we've worked out an agreement for the Romanian contingent of Piranha-5s to be put on loan to us.

"And as we speak, Lt. Colonel Michaud's people are getting the low down on how to make those beauties work. Between the Piranhas and their 30mm cannons and our own G-Wagons, we'll have more than enough firepower if we get into the shit."

A smile beamed onto the CDS's face. "The Romanians are solid, and we've been good to them. Nicely played, Nate. What else?"

"That Global Affairs Canada quick reaction team we put together a few years ago has paid off in spades. I'm not sure how they did it, but the folks at GAC got permission for us to land a six-pack of Super Hornets, a Super Heron, and all the kit that's needed for forward operations at the Grace Bay airport in Turks and Caicos. By midnight, we'll be able to offer a full range of surveillance and ground support options should we need them."

The CDS's greying eyebrows elevated. "Right, the Turks and Caicos. I remember some talk about them becoming a province back in the day. God, when was that?"

"The last time it was talked about with any seriousness was back when Harper was PM, some twenty years ago. It didn't go anywhere but they're closer to us now than they ever were to the British," Hermes explained.

"And what about the Brits? Have we brought them into this yet? If memory serves they have assets in this neck of the woods."

"They do," Hermes advised soberly, "and the most important of these is a SIGINT outfit on the Virgin Islands. We'd like to see its full bandwidth directed at several people in Port-au-Prince - we're talking to the right people in the UK government as we speak to make that happen. Our SIGINT folks have been probing that part of the world all morning, but it's a challenge due to the distances involved. Once the Brits come on board, we should get more of what we need."

"Nice. I'm curious to see how robust this new CANZUK agreement is. With the world getting more crazy by the day, I suspect His Majesty's Government will be eager to help us along. With the way things are shaping up in the US, the four of us are gonna have to work a bit harder at supporting one another for the foreseeable future."

"Agreed," said Hermes. "The CANZUK deal has potential, but if this op moves forward it'll be fast and it'll be us and only us."

"As it must be if we're going to pull this off. Now, what's the plan?"

Hermes looked to his left and locked eyes with one of his senior planning officers. "Claire put it on the display."

Standing, Hermes moved in front of the huge display hanging on the wall behind him. The screen generated a map of Haiti, which then quickly transitioned into the cityscape of Port-au-Prince. With two hands, Hermes manipulated the map so that it featured a brown field with the markings of a soccer pitch. "This is where the Vandoos were ambushed at around 0730 hours this morning." Again, he manipulated the map. When it resolved, the satellite image at the center of the display showed a three-building compound with faded orange-clay roofs.

"This is Alpha-7's headquarters. It's about five klicks east of the ambush location. At this time, we can't say if the captain is still here but, in the next few hours, we'll have the right people on the ground, we'll have eyes in the sky, and we'll have all the SIGINT we can handle, and all of it will be focused on this location like a laser. By the time JTF-2 is in country, we'll be as certain as we can be that this is where they're holding her."

"Terrific work, Nate. The PM said whatever you need, you can have. She's as determined as we are to see Bertrand pulled out of this nightmare, so if she needs to take a political hit for you to make that happen, she's prepared to do that."

"Good to know, sir. Cause as best we can tell, this Alpha-7 outfit is no joke. The attack they undertook today was well-planned and well-executed. And as we all know too well, they're prepared to kill.

"But as it was for them this morning, surprise is now with us. Whatever the motivations for today's attack, the leadership of Alpha-7 will be expecting us to undertake several days, even weeks, of negotiations to get Bertrand back. It's what everyone expects. As a country, it's what we do."

Hermes again tapped the display and the video image of six Canadian soldiers lying dead on a dirt field confronted the collection of senior officers who had gathered in the main operations room near the centre of Canada's National Defence Headquarters. As they took in the macabre scene, a dog trotted into the now two-hour old footage and began to smell and then lick one of the prone bodies. Soon, it was joined by another and then another. Hermes stopped the video and froze the image.

"Sir, it's imperative that the PM and GAC give the impression that we want a negotiated solution. Give the Alpha-7s and the rest of the world every reason to think that we're going to handle this like the polite middle power that we are. Because when we're on the ground, as soon as we hear the word 'go', we're gonna crack open that shithole of a compound, we're going to take our officer back, and we're going to bring her home."

Chapter 3

Port-au-Prince

Petit had left the meeting at the hotel with his Haitian government contact feeling like he had a better handle on Alpha-7. It was the city's largest and most powerful gang and was led by a former army officer – one Peterson Dorvil. By all accounts, it was said he was a calculating man who preferred using bribes and blackmail instead of brute force. Which made the brashness of the morning's attack all the more difficult to understand. Why attack and execute UN soldiers? he asked himself, not for the first time that morning.

The answer lay behind the eyes of the goblin-like man presently on his display. Emmanuel 'Face' Jean was the nephew of Dorvil and was the man who had exposed his face in the moments before the Vandoos were executed.

His bureaucratic contact from the hotel earlier that morning had advised Jean was one of three senior captains in the Sevens and that he did a lot of the nasty hands-on work the gang still needed to do from time to time.

Petit pushed back from his desk still looking at the man on his display. Was it a power play? Maybe the attack was the result of some internal struggle between Jean and his boss. The file on Dorvil said the leader of the Alpha-7s was sixty-one years old. As gangsters went in a country like Haiti, that was well into the territory of ancient.

If it wasn't sanctioned by Dorvil, the morning's attack could upset the apple cart within the gang. It would be the cautious and comfortable old man versus the hungry and entrepreneurial upstart. Both would have their supporters. Maybe this morning's play was a brazen effort by Jean to swing support his way? Petit rationalized. But executing UN soldiers and taking responsibility for it was one hell of a way to tell your boss you're not happy with his leadership.

As he continued to take in the homely image of the man that had just killed eleven of his country's soldiers, he said aloud, "If it's not a power play then what the hell is going on?"

It was just another of the many questions he had without answers. The challenge was that he didn't have the luxury of time to let the info percolate up through the city's endless ranks of criminals and corrupt officials. The message he'd received from Ottawa had been explicit: "MOTIVATION/DRIVING FACTORS FOR MORNING'S AT-TACK NEEDED WITHIN 24 HOURS. ALL OPTIONS ARE IN PLAY TO OBTAIN INFO. REPORT IN EVERY FOUR HOURS."

In grand total, the CSIS had three field officers in Haiti and he hadn't seen Drapeau and Lachance all morning. They would have their own tasks, of course. In his case, he had been given nineteen hours to solve the mystery that was Canada's most serious foreign policy crisis in at least a generation. It was a tall order, but he was a resourceful man, and his country had just given him a blank cheque.

———

Jacmel, Haiti

As he deplaned from the BN2 Islander, Baptiste took in a deep breath through his nose. Unlike the air in Port-Au-Prince, the south-ernmost coast of the country smelled of the ocean and at the moment, the breeze had a slight floral tinge to it. It was intoxicating.

It had been four years since he'd last been in Haiti. His wife's only sister and the only sibling who hadn't emigrated to Canada had been on her deathbed. She had asked for her older sister to come to her side and Jenelle had heeded the call. Despite looking like death had already taken her, the stubborn woman had taken nearly two weeks to pass. In that time, Baptiste had seen more of Port-au-Prince than he cared to re-member.

Yes, there were lovely and kind people throughout the city, and parts of the capital were delightful with its French colonial architecture, and its mix of languages, but the unforgiving rot of the city's corruption was never far away.

His parents had fled the country for Canada when he was five and while he held a Haitian passport and could switch over to Creole as he needed, he did not consider himself Haitian. His parents had left this backward and broken country for the promise of a better life and each of their four children had fulfilled that promise. At forty-four, and after twenty-five years in the CAF, he was as Canadian as maple syrup, full stop.

He turned and took in the two younger men that CANSOFCOM had assigned to him. While he had reminisced, the two well-built soldiers had gathered up the five large bags they had between them. Dressed in clothing that Baptiste was confident would pass as civie-enough for the amount of time they were planning to be here, there was no hiding their obvious fitness. By and large, Haitian men didn't work out, for no other reason than that Port-au-Prince had a dearth of gyms. Compared to the average man who would be walking the city streets of Haiti's capital, the two men standing in front of him would catch their fair share of looks. Broad shoulders and thick necks did that in a country dominated by destitution.

He stretched out one of his hands and said, "Here, Ady, give me one of those." The thick six-three Haitian-Canadian army reservist unofficially on loan from the Montreal Police's drug squad grunted and tossed Baptiste one of the three bags he was carrying. "It's all yours, old man. If it starts to weigh you down, just let me know."

As he caught the heavy bag, Baptiste smiled at the younger man's jibe, but said nothing.

He turned to the other man who was carrying their remaining two bags. He was a touch shorter than the Montrealer and had dark brown skin. Sergeant Blake Cole was a four-year veteran of JTF-2 and was a born-and-bred product of Toronto. His French was shit, and he wouldn't fool anyone trying to pass himself off as Haitian, but if all went to plan, the block of a man wouldn't need to speak a word of the language. Cole, a mission specialist, would operate the collection of drones they had brought with them and if needed, he could blow things up with the ample supply of explosives he was lugging.

"You ready for this?" asked Baptiste.

"Aces, Bap. I was made for this shit. Let's get this party started."

Baptiste saw Coles' eyes shift past him in the direction of the tarmac that stretched toward the small airport's terminal. Turning, he took in a man walking towards them who on quick inspection appeared to be a local. But as soon as he spoke, the man's too-strong Quebecois accent made it clear who he was.

The man was neither tall nor short and though there was a slight pudge to him, Baptiste suspected the softness was more due to a combination of age and too much desk work than it was a life of idleness. At some point, the man had lifted. As he reached them, he confidently jutted out his hand and delivered a firm handshake.

"Mr. Baptiste. My name is Drapeau. Welcome to Haiti, sir. I have it on good authority that you're familiar with many of the wonders and secrets that this lovely country has to offer. I have been asked to assist you in whatever way you might need."

"Mr. Drapeau, good of you to come and meet us. We plan to keep you busy over the next day or so. You have transportation?"

"I do. Out front. Two four-by-fours, as requested."

"Good stuff. Let's get going then. We need to be in Petion-Ville in three hours."

"Not impossible, but we'll have to move fast," Drapeau said as he began to follow Baptiste in the direction of the terminal and the foursome's waiting vehicles.

Striding forward, Baptiste easily hoisted the duffle bag Ady had given to him over his shoulder and said, "I like that, Mr. Drapeau. 'Not impossible.' With your help, there will be a lot of 'not impossible' happening over the next twenty-four hours or so."

The Alpha-7 Compound, Port-au-Prince

Bertrand suspected she was in a basement. There were no windows, and the room was dank. If she had to guess, she had been here for eight hours or so, but the absence of natural light made it impossible to tell. A single bulb in the ceiling left the extremities of the space dark, giving the room a foreboding feel reminiscent of a 70s-era slasher flick.

She had cried only once, and then only after the second beating where they had touched her. It had not been the man who had taken off his mask at the field where her men had been slaughtered, but a pair of underlings who she had suspected had skulked down to wherever she was to have some unapproved fun. At the beginning, she had screamed and told them to fuck off and for a brief moment that had given her the power to resist. But that feeling had been fleeting and there were two of them.

Mercifully, they had not taken long. As her tongue prodded a pair of too-loose teeth at the front of her mouth, she resolved to concentrate on their faces. To burn their individual faces into her mind so that when it came time to identify them, her recollection would be crystal clear. This gave her the power to endure.

As she lay quietly on a filthy single mattress, the room's only physical item, her mind ran through the occasions that she was aware of when Canadians had been taken as hostages abroad. Months, and in some cases, years, these men or women had suffered confinement and horrific abuse. And in each case, Canada, a middling entity with little to no hard-power options, had done little to help its citizens. Would it make a difference that she was a soldier? Would it make a difference that Haiti was not China? To what lengths would Canada put her safety and freedom over its standing in the feckless body that was the UN? These and many other questions flitted through her mind as she endeavored to stave off what had happened to her.

Despite the inherent bleakness of the questions, she did have hope. She was certain she was still in Port-au-Prince, and she knew that Canada would have the image of the man who had led the attack on her convoy. Once, long before her time as a soldier, Canada had been a country of action. The Somme, Dieppe, Afghanistan. In those conflicts, the country had understood the cost of conflict but had made the sacrifice all the same. That knowledge and the hope it inspired was something, so she clung to it like a blanket as she lay there in the desolate silence and waited for what would come next

Chapter 4

Ottawa

Bahir loved his job almost as much as he loved his country. He had come to Canada as a refugee, and now, twenty-three years later, he held a Ph.D. in computer science from UBC and was managing a team of hackers or 'cyber warfare specialists,' as was their official designation within the Canadian Security Establishment – CSE – Canada's much smaller, but nearly as capable version of the Americans' NSA.

Like all Canadians, he had been outraged by the high-def drone video footage that had leaked out of the UN earlier in the day. As he laid down another line of code, he pictured the pair of masked brutes dragging away the female officer from the soldiers she had just seen murdered.

Three hours ago, his boss had provided him with six names, and he'd been told in no uncertain terms that his team should drop what they were doing and scour whatever part of the internet they needed to build a profile on, and gain leverage over, the six named persons.

Unsurprisingly, five of the names were Haitians residing in Haiti. Getting intel on those folks should be relatively straightforward for those team members he had assigned the task. For the most part, Haiti's cyber-infrastructure was a joke compared to Western or Chinese standards. He had kept the Irishman for himself.

Unlike Haiti, European citizens benefited from a robust cyber-network that had redundancies galore and encrypted components designed to stymie and outright deny people like Bahir and his unit. But no matter a network's sophistication, there was always the chance the end-user did something that would give a talented and determined operator a way to get what they wanted. Too often, people were some combination of careless or stupid when it came to protecting their data. To his credit, Major General Micheal O'Regan of the Irish Army was

33

not one of those people. His eldest son on the other hand... well, he had
not been nearly as careful.

––––––

The National Palace, Port-au-Prince

She had not taken much convincing. Blank cheques were just that,
and Petit had leveraged the full weight of his new authority to offer a
deal that the beautiful young woman beside him could not say no to.
Instant immigration to Canada for her, her two-year-old daughter, her
mother, and six years of payments to get her through university and beyond in her new country. Hell, without question, he would have said
yes to that deal if he were in her shoes.

The car they were riding in pulled up to the security gates of Haiti's
newly reconstructed presidential palace. Badly damaged in the devas-
tating 2010 earthquake, it had taken just over two decades to fully re-
build the expansive property.

"Miss Vanessa," the delighted policeman from Haiti's national police force said to the woman driving the vehicle. "Working on the weekend, I see?"

"Yes, Junior. Just for a bit, though."

The guard's face switched from sweet to sour when his eyes fell on
Petit, his right hand casually lying along the pistol grip of the weathered
HK MP5 hanging from a strap over his shoulders. "And who's your
friend?"

"This is my uncle. He's from Cap-Haitien. He's down here on business. I was hoping I could show him my office and a few other places
on the grounds? He's a huge admirer of President Laurent."

The young policeman's brow furrowed and he tsked, a sound of an-
noyance common among the country's working class. "You know the
rules, Miss Vanessa. No one who isn't pre-approved gets in. I'm sorry,
but it's the rules."

"I know the rules, Junior, but I was hoping we could make an exception for me and just for today. My uncle is leaving town first thing

tomorrow and he's not sure when he'll next be back." As she made her plea, her hand went to a pendant hanging in the cleavage of her breasts. Petit watched the guard watch the woman beside him with an unchecked hunger. For pity's sake, he thought, were men always this predictable?

"I'll tell you what," Vanessa said, her voice almost a purr. "If you do this favor for me, I'll let you take me for that drink you've been talking about for the past year. Nothing more mind you – just a drink."

On hearing the offer, the man's eyes lit up like a Christmas tree, but just as quickly, they narrowed. "Oh, Ms. Vanessa, it's a kind offer you are making, but I could lose my job if I let your uncle in. There's something going on today. Lots of important people are coming and going. If I did you this favor, I'd be taking on a big risk. A big risk. My parents. If I don't send them money, I couldn't live with myself. I mean, a drink with you would be nice, but..."

The trailing off of the man's words was a signal to Vanessa to raise her ante, but Petit would have none of it. He was heaping enough risk on this woman already without her having to commit her body to the cause.

"Listen my friend," he interjected. "Let me help you both out. You're both young and drinks in the big city aren't free." Petit reached into the front pocket of his shirt and pulled out a money clip. Slowly, he counted off several American bills and held them in front of the woman's chest. The guard's eyes went from the woman's cleavage to the bills and then back again to her ample breasts.

Just as the leering was becoming too much, the policeman's eyes snapped upwards and locked onto Petit's face. "What's your name?"

Returning the other man's stare, Petit said, "Ronnie Jean-Pierre."

The guard muttered something under his breath and then quickly turned away from the car and walked in the direction of the guard-house, where another member of the Haitian National Police had been standing, watching their interaction.

"Should we leave?" Vanessa said, her voice low.

"No. Keep doing what you're doing. You're a natural," Petit said with what he hoped was a kind smile.

After what seemed like an interminable amount of time, the policeman stepped out of the guardhouse and made his way back to their car. As he walked, his face was impassive.

Reaching the driver's side of the vehicle, he leaned in close to the open window and then reached in with his left hand and handed Petit a sticker that had the word "Visiteur" in bold letters across the front of it.

"Put this on. I've registered you in the system, Mr. Jean-Pierre. Don't go anywhere you shouldn't. Ms. Vanessa knows the rules." A smile leaped to his face as he said her name.

Petit took the sticker and then moved to give the man the money.

"No. Not me. Give it to her," the guard said while waving his hand at the money. "She can give it to me when we go for that drink she just promised. I know she is good for it."

Vanessa flashed her terrific smile at the policeman. "When I next see you, I'll give you a time when we can get together. I promise, Junior."

The man's smile was now a bonfire of joy. "I'm here all week, Ms. Vanessa. Just let me know when and where."

The guard stepped back from their car and gave a signal to the man in the guardhouse. As the heavy steel gate began to open, Petit allowed himself to exhale deeply.

"Well done, Ms. Vanessa."

The administrative secretary for Haiti's Minister of Justice and Public Security looked at him. In that moment, she was as striking a woman as he had ever seen.

"Just get me, my baby, and mom, out of this place. The sooner, the better."

———

The Toussaint Louverture International Airport

From the tarmac, Lt. Colonel Michaud had watched both of the Royal Canadian Air Force Airbus CC-150 Polaris land and taxi as close as they could get to the hangar that had been assigned to the UN mission at the airport.

It was 2200 hours, so the chances that an enterprising reporter would be lurking around this part of the airport to take pictures of the unloading soldiers was low.

The loose lips of the locals that worked at the airport and the military staff from the various countries that made up the UN contingent were an entirely different challenge and not one he had the time or resources to address. Within an hour of JTF-2 emerging from the two airliners laid out in front of him, all of the right people in this city would know about it, starting with O'Regan.

When he did get the word, the Irish general would be incensed. Though a self-serving bureaucrat, the man was no fool. The moment he laid eyes on the hulking soldiers and their specialized kit, he would put two and two together and calls would be made to the UN, the EU, the media, and anyone else who might play a part in throwing up roadblocks to whatever action the Canadian government might want to take.

Michaud could see it now – after calling for an emergency debate, the Chinese and Russian ambassadors would lecture anyone that would listen that Canada, America's long-time lackey, was violating the terms of its participation in the Haiti mission and that a UN-led investigation would be undertaken to look into the deaths of Canada's soldiers and that Captain Bertrand would be allowed to return home in good time. And while this predictable bureaucratic two-step was underway in New York, here in Haiti, O'Regan would smugly make it his personal mission to make sure Canada followed each and every step and process that was unhurriedly dolled out by the Security Council over the next several weeks. As he thought about the bookish-looking Irishman, Michaud's jaw clenched.

As the door to the closest plane opened, the first of the onboard soldiers stepped out of the entrance. The Canadian Army's officer corps was a small community, so he instantly recognized the man who had started to make his way down the airstairs. As the officer's boots hit the pavement of the tarmac, Michaud snapped a crisp salute.

"Sir, welcome to Haiti."

"Mich, good to see you. I'm glad it's you here. I'm sorry about your boys."

"I'm sorry, too. It's a shit situation, Gord. I'm hoping you'll be able to share some details about what our next steps are. As you can imagine, my group is chomping at the bit. If there are plans brewing to get back Bertrand, we want to be part of it."

"I'll read you in as soon as I can, but first things first, we need to find General O'Regan. Where is he?

"Mission headquarters would be my guess. He'll be furious when he finds out about you, but I guess there's no help for that," said Michaud.

Colonel Gordon McCord, commander of JTF-2, Canada's tier-one special operations outfit, looked over Michaud's shoulder back into the bowels of the hanger. "That's an affirmative on the fury Mich. That's one pissed-off-looking Irishman. I didn't know they could get that red."

Michaud turned and immediately took in O'Regan striding toward them. He was flanked by two other officers: his second-in-command – a colonel from the Irish Army – and a Chilean major with whom Michaud got along. He had thought they would get at least an hour before the glowering man got word of McCord's arrival, but that estimate had been woefully incorrect.

As they took in the threesome of approaching officers, the special operations commander asked, "Is there a room in this place that we can grab quickly? I'll need to speak privately with him."

"There's a couple of offices in the back that I can get access to," said Michaud just as O'Regan arrived at their location.

"And just who might we have here, Lt. Colonel Michaud? And why the hell wasn't I advised that your government was flying in these planes?"

McCord stepped forward. A tall, strapping man who had at least half a foot in height over O'Regan, he gave the UN mission commander a parade ground-worthy salute.

"Sir, my name is Colonel Gordon McCord. Sorry to have to meet under such extraordinary circumstances. If you'll come with me, Lt. Colonel Michaud will show us to a room where I can give you a quick overview of why I'm here."

The general shot McCord a withering stare. "Come with you? I won't do anything of the sort, Colonel. You will tell me why you're here, and you will tell me now. I can see soldiers on these planes of yours. I can tell you that under no circumstances will they be setting foot in this country. Under UN Resolution 3012, no country participating in this mission is permitted to add additional forces without the express permission of the Security Council. I checked my messages before leaving the compound, Colonel McCord, and I can assure you that there was no message from New York advising me of your arrival. Of all countries, I'm surprised that Canada has so brazenly disregarded the will of the UN by sending you here. I'm sorry you've wasted your time. Whatever your reasons for being here, they don't concern me or the UN mission. My suggestion is that you turn around, get back on that plane of yours and go back where you came from."

As the words left the Irishman's mouth, Michaud heard a clanking sound coming from the direction of the same aircraft McCord had deplaned from. Shifting his eyes in that direction, he took in a dozen or so fully armed soldiers making their way down the airstairs.

They were a menacing sight. Each soldier appeared to be supremely fit and was kitted up in full battle armor, including the distinctive-looking helmets worn exclusively by Canada's special forces community. Each man also had several weapons on their person. Perhaps half of them were carrying the latest version of the American M-4 rifle while several others were sporting the bullpup Fabrique Nationale P-90. All weapons were fitted with suppressors and night vision kit abounded. As the group of soldiers arrived at their location, they formed a loose circle around McCord, O'Regan, and the rest of the officers.

O'Regan ignored the soldiers and stared imperiously at McCord. "This is outrageous. I will not be intimidated by you or your thugs, Colonel. The Security Council and international law is on my side. See yourselves away now, and I'll see that this pathetic intimidation tactic doesn't make it into my report back to New York."

McCord took half a step toward the Irish general and towered over the man. He lowered his voice and said something that Michaud couldn't make out and then the Canadian special forces commander handed the other man a tactical pad. O'Regan looked at the unit's display and then after several seconds of reading its contents, said aloud, "Five minutes, Colonel. You have five minutes before I make a call to UN Headquarters to blow the top off whatever shite game your country is up to."

Chapter 5

Port-au-Prince

Looking west, Baptiste took in the beginnings of what would be the standard glorious Caribbean sunset. Warm oranges dabbled the clouds actively running cover for the declining sun. Taking one last look, he climbed down from the last telephone pole he would need to ascend during what had been a productive six hours.

Reaching the decrepit asphalt, he glanced at the CSIS agent who was sitting in the driver's seat of the orange-and-blue NATCOM mini-van he had somehow got his hands on. Drapeau flashed a thumbs-up signaling that the unit he had just installed was operational.

The installation of the units across this part of the city hadn't been difficult work. Although most Haitians communicated via cell phone, in Port-au-Prince, the demand for internet connectivity was constant, so NATCOM vehicles were a ubiquitous sight across the city installing or fixing the maze of ugly cabling that snaked through every neighborhood. For the locals, his installation of the small, nondescript black boxes near the top of nine different spires was an entirely unremarkable event.

He opened the passenger door and plunked himself onto the heavily stained seat. Without saying a word, Drapeau hit the gas, sending the vehicle forward.

"Where to, boss?" Drapeau said.

"The soccer field."

Twenty minutes later, their van pulled into the dusty open space that served as the parking lot for the soccer field where the five Canadians had been executed thirteen hours ago. Unsurprisingly, a group of teenaged boys were on the field and were fully engaged in the beautiful game. More than a few weren't wearing shoes.

Had they known about the dead soldiers from earlier in the day? Probably not, reasoned Baptiste. At fourteen, you didn't care about dead soldiers from other countries nearly as much as you did about playing soccer and chasing girls. Whatever anger he held toward the kids running about the field, he shunted away. There were others in this cursed city who were a much better fit for the emotions he was feeling in that moment.

Turning his eyes from the game, he took in the on-loan Montreal police officer/reservist and the JTF-2 soldier. Together, the two men were casually leaning back against the beaten-up Toyota 4Runner that the CSIS operative had secured for them.

"Nice ride," said Ady as Baptiste arrived at their location.

"It ain't pretty and it smells like shit inside, but we could go anywhere, no questions asked," Baptiste said. "Any issues on your end?"

It was Cole who responded. "We could only set up three of the five locations. Too many people around at the other two."

"That's all we needed. What about the old man? He's good?"

"He's good," replied Ady. "He's not a fan of the gangs and this Alpha-7 group is number one on his shit list."

"You're sure he can be trusted, then?" said Baptiste.

"He's good, boss. The man is family and even if he wasn't, you could see it in his eyes. He hates the gangs. He hasn't forgotten what they did to his grandson. The pain is just under the surface and it's real. I can feel it when he speaks. He hates these bastards more than we ever could. Whatever he can do for us, he'll do it."

Baptiste held out his fist to fist bump the big Montrealer. "Alright, so we got a place to lie low for the next few hours. Good work, Ady. I just got word that McCord and his boys are set to land. There's a good chance we do this early morning. Drapeau and I will lose the van and then we'll meet you back at the old man's place. We wait there until we get the call."

"Wait," said Drapeau. "Who's this McCord fellow and who are his boys? I'm up to my neck in it now, so you better read me in."

It was Cole who replied. "Some bad motherfuckers are about to set down in this city you keep trying to up sell us on. And McCord is bad man numero uno. Shit is about to get real, Draps."

Drapeau turned to face Baptiste. "Care to translate?"

Baptiste smiled. "What Sergeant Cole just said was that JTF-2 will be on the ground in the hour and on the second part, his assessment is most certainly correct – shit is about to get real, real damned fast."

The Alpha-7 Compound

Bertrand could see natural light through the blindfold, and hear the sound of chirping birds through open windows. Her own sense of time told her it was close to the end of the day, but somewhere close by, someone was brewing coffee. It smelled like a miracle. Wherever she was, it wasn't a basement.

"Remove it," said a deep voice.

From behind her, someone roughly fiddled with the fabric tied at the back of her head, and then all of the sudden she could see. The glare of natural light forced her to squint but after several seconds, her vision adjusted, allowing her to take in the scene in front of her.

She was in a large study or office of some sort. At the center of the room was a massive wooden desk. It was neatly organized with several sheaves of paper and a few books. A large man with greying hair and a kindly-looking face sat behind the desk looking at her. Standing to his right was the man from the soccer field. His eyes were no longer crazed and as he returned her gaze, there was no hint of malice or anger on his soft face. Something else was there now – chastened, perhaps?

"Would you like a drink?" said the seated older man. As he said the words, he pointed to her right.

She followed his gesture and took in a set of oversized glass double doors that led onto an expansive balcony, where there was a modest-looking iron-wrought table, a pair of chairs, and a single, oversized, red umbrella. On the table was a tall, glistening pitcher of water. She was terribly thirsty.

"Yes, I'll have a drink," she said.

"Good. Antoine, would you fetch our guest a glass of water."

His hand moved and gestured to a chair in front of the desk. "Please, Captain. Have a seat."

Her hands still bound, she moved forward and lowered herself into the waiting chair.

A man, presumably Antoine, then walked into her vision and gently placed the tall, cool glass in her hands. She accepted it and without hesitation or grace, downed the first half of the cool liquid, triggering relief in that part of her brain dedicated to her survival.

"Better?" the man asked.

"Yes, thank you."

He smiled at her reply.

"Captain Bertrand, I – we – owe you an apology."

Upon saying the words, the man looked past her. Behind her, she heard a door open, and the sound of footfalls and cursing filled her ears. After a few seconds, two men with bound hands had been marched into the room in front of another pair of men. The foursome stopped to the right of the old man's desk and turned so that she could see all their faces.

The two men in front were the two that had hurt her a few hours earlier. Both men had distressed looks on their faces and their eyes darted around the room as though they were cornered rats. Though they were not close to her and the space was airy, she was able to catch the smell of stale tobacco emanating from the pair. She would never forget that smell. Her stomach suddenly roiled, signaling that she might have to vomit.

The old man's baritone voice pulled her away from the brewing reaction in her body. "These men, Captain. They did something to you, did they not?"

It took a moment for Bertrand to process the question, but then the scene before her began to make sense. As the penny dropped, she delivered her reply, injecting a hint of venom into her voice. "Yes."

After a pause and a deep exhalation, the man who must have been the leader of the Alpha-7s said, "I am sorry it is so."

The old man canted his head to his left. "These are two of my nephew's men and like my nephew, they can sometimes get carried away. I did not approve nor do I like what they did to you. It is... uncivilized."

Upon saying those words, the two guards standing behind her two attackers simultaneously kicked at the back of their legs forcing them to their knees. Then both men reached behind their backs and produced semi-automatic pistols, which they aimed at the back of each man's head. They held the weapons steady and waited.

"For reasons that I suspect will become clear to you in the coming weeks, we had to undertake the unpleasant business that involved your men. Haiti is tired of other governments trying to run our affairs. In a short time, a new government - a government of the people, will be sending that same message to the international community. I regret that your men had to die so that my country could send that message. In their case, there is nothing I can do. But as to what you experienced in my own home, well, that is something I can address."

The man shifted in his chair, opening his body to the left. Looking at the two armed henchmen, he said, "Do it."

As the words left his mouth, the two men shifted their pistols away from the kneeling men and pointed them in the direction of the Alpha-7 leader. Without a word, gunshots filled the room. Bertrand flinched and watched in horror as the seated man with the kind voice bucked violently as multiple high-velocity bullets entered his chest, each of the rounds spewing globs of bright red blood as they penetrated deep into flesh.

Only when each assassin had emptied his respective weapon's magazine did they stop firing. As they lowered their weapons, the grievously wounded man took in ragged breaths, slumped forward, and collapsed onto the marbled floor.

Ugly as ever, Jean strode forward from where he had been standing to lord over the gasping man. His face was pasted with the same smile he had worn earlier in the day on the soccer field. Lazily, he raised his right hand and pointed his own pistol in the direction of the prone man's head and without saying a word, pulled the trigger.

In that instant, the sound of the kill shot wiped away whatever hope she had been feeling only seconds before.

Slowly, Jean turned to Bertrand, his eyes once again filled with loathing. He smiled to reveal his yellow teeth and walked toward her. He stopped in front of her and raised his gun, pointing it at her face.

"We apologize for nothing," the man said in a low growl. "Things are about to change in this country, and you and what happened to your men today will serve as a warning to others that the new Haiti will not be cowed, bought, or dictated to. Haiti is strong, my lovely captain. Strong enough to do what was done today and more if it is needed. You'll see."

He turned away from her and looked at the other men in the room. "Untie them. You two swine get to live, but let this be a lesson to you. When it comes to as precious a prize as our guest here, you don't get to touch without my permission. Tell the others – no one so much as looks at her without my say-so. Understood?"

"Yeah, boss," the two men said simultaneously.

"Good, then get the fuck out of here."

As the two thugs scurried from the room, the new leader of the Alpha-7s addressed the remaining men. "Clean her up and feed her. If I'm feeling up to it, I'll pay her a visit tonight."

The National Palace, Port-au-Prince

Once past the outer gates, Vanessa had parked her car and absent Petit had walked to that part of the building where her office was located.

Upon receiving a text from her, Petit had strolled to a sub-surface loading dock on the backside of the newly finished building. Wearing a pair of grey overalls, a pasted-on mustache, and carrying a satchel with various tools, he walked through the door that the young woman was holding open for him.

Being freshly constructed, Petit knew that the national palace had cameras everywhere, but according to Vanessa and other sources, there were only ever two guards managing the CCTV system. With hundreds of cameras to keep an eye on, the chances that he would be spotted entering the building were slim to none. And with parts of the building still being finalized, he hoped his disguise would give him enough play that he could get to the areas he needed to. The building was busier than it should have been on a Saturday afternoon, but the attack on the convoy and the subsequent soccer field massacre had transformed the building into a beehive of activity. He would just have to make it work.

Inside the building, he turned back to his newly converted asset. "Thanks for everything, Van. My country owes you, and I owe you."

"Yeah, well, you offered a deal I couldn't refuse. I love this country, but it just can't seem to get its shit together, you know. It's not a place where I want my daughter to grow up. The things I had to do just to get this job. I'm sick of it. All of it. I'm better than this. My baby is better than this."

She looked at him with the rarest set of amber eyes. She had full lips and the most wonderful curves. They had met several months ago, and in that time, he had been building a relationship with her with the hope that he would be able to turn her into a formal asset. But today's events had dramatically altered his timeline. Based on a hunch, and with a figurative blank check in hand, he had rolled the dice, hoping she would choose to help his country.

He reached out and took her hand. "Keep an eye on your phone. If something happens to me, get yourself out of here, and get to Jacmel as quietly and as soon as you can. The man there – Lachance – he'll make sure you get out of the country."

"I know, we've been through the options a dozen times. My baby can't afford for me to spend the rest of my life in jail. One way or another, I'm going to get out of this city, and then I'm going to get my family out of this country. It's what you promised."

"Exactly," said the CSIS officer.

Her other hand went to the pendant on her chest. "When this is done, you'll find me, right?"

"I'll find you. Trust me," Petit said while squeezing her hand gently.

"I do trust you. I have to."

With that, she gently pulled her hand from his, turned and began to walk down the hallway. After a dozen steps, she stopped and turned back to look at him. Her fetching eyes shone even at this distance. "Promise me that when you find me, you'll tell me your real name. You've never really struck me as a Ronnie."

Smiling, Petit said without hesitation, "I promise that too."

She offered nothing in response. After a long moment, her eyes left him, she turned and resumed her departure. As he watched her go, he seared his memory with the mesmerizing sway of the woman's perfect hips. Back home, Petit would make whatever had just happened between them into something more. But to do that, he had to complete his assignment and then survive whatever was to come in the next few hours.

Where Vanessa had turned the corner, Petit kept walking down an extended corridor where he eventually made his own turn. By luck or by chance, the building's server room was on this floor and close by. He walked by several rooms that had open doors. Most were larger offices with several cubicles in them. The worker bees had been stuck in the basement – no surprise there. What was a surprise was that he hadn't seen a single person. Whatever political maneuvering was being done by the Haitian government on the floors above clearly didn't require the assistance of the day-to-day administrative staff. Turning a corner, he approached the first door on the right. The sign on the door read 'Restricted Access'.

From his satchel, he pulled out a small device and held it to the keypad on the door. After a second, the door clicked, and he pushed it open.

The room held a bank of servers. Like the rest of the building, the machines appeared to be new. Each of the units was festooned with various lights and glowing LCD panels. As a part of his training, he had been taught how to navigate the real estate of a server and a few hours earlier, via an encrypted link, he had watched and taken notes as a tech from the CSE had given him an impromptu tutorial on what he needed to do from a similar-looking room somewhere in Ottawa.

He again reached into his satchel and pulled out a device that looked like a USB and a small tablet. Standing in front of the last server in the row, he inserted the USB into one of the ports and then hit the unit's power button. The lights on the unit flickered and went dead. As he pressed the power button to restart the server, he heard a click at the door. Instantly, he stashed the tablet back in the satchel and turned to face whoever was coming into the room.

The door opened and Petit stood face-to-face with a man who looked to be his own age and height. But where Petit was fit to the point it was too frequently commented on, the man in front of him sported a good-sized paunch and an overall softness that suggested he spent way too much time behind a keyboard. The man took a step into the room and positioned himself in such a way to block the door from closing on its pneumatic hinge.

For whatever reason, the server tech – if that's who he was – didn't seem surprised to see him standing there. After briefly taking in Petit's face, the man's dark eyes moved to his overalls and the various tools protruding out of his satchel.

"What are you doing in here?" the man asked with a sharp tone.

Prepared with a story, Petit delivered an immediate reply. "My supervisor sent me down to check out one of the outlets. We got a complaint there was some surging taking place. It looks like everything is good, though."

"I run the servers in this place," the man said, making no effort to hide the agitation in his voice. "No one told me about any power issues. Who's your supervisor and where's your ID? You should have it on display at all times. Stupid contractors. You guys walk around here like you think you own the place. Well, you don't."

The man put his hands on his hips and glowered at Petit. "Well? What's the story, or do I need to call security?"

"ID, ah... hold on. I got it right here," said Petit as his left-hand dove deep into one of his pockets. Pulling out an empty hand, he took a step toward the technician, holding up his palm.

The man looked at his empty hand and then locked eyes with Petit. "Is this a joke?"

Petit struck like a viper, hammering the other man in his solar plexus with a balled fist. The tech grunted as the force of the blow ejected all of the air out of his lungs. As the gasping man fell to his knees, Petit pivoted behind him and kicked him forward. As the door began to close, Petit walked in the direction of the now sprawled-out technician.

As he stared down at the tech, in his mind's eye he replayed the video of his fellow countrymen being filled with bullets on that filthy patch of dirt and of the female officer being struck by that maskless animal Jean.

Still gasping for breath, the technician had managed to get on his hands and knees. Through ragged, shallow breaths, Petit heard the man try to mumble words. Stepping forward, he reached down and grabbed the back of the man's shirt and with five-hundred-pound dead-lift strength, he hauled the technician to his feet. Erect, Petit put the man in a rear-naked choke, and with vice-like strength, slowly snuffed the life out of the soft man who had the misfortune of interrupting his work.

Waiting a full thirty seconds after the man's last indication of movement, Petit gently lowered the tech to the floor and positioned him in such a way that it looked like he might have suffered a heart attack. Turning back to the server, he pulled out the tablet and after moving through several options, he initiated the process that would allow several teams of Canada's most seasoned cyber warfare operators to storm through the Haitian government's most sensitive data.

His tablet flashed a message that the data link had been secured. He removed the data stick from the server panel and placed it and the tablet back in his tool satchel. He did not look in the direction of the man he had just killed. Instead, he turned toward the room's entrance. Reaching the door, he opened it slowly and peered into the hallway. As before, it was empty.

With his heart pounding in his chest, Petit stepped out of the room and walked in the direction from which he had come. As he forced himself to travel the long white hallway at a normal pace, he made an effort to project an air of confidence that would signal to whatever person he encountered next that he had every right to be where he was.

As he arrived at the same entrance he had used to enter the building, he pulled out his phone and sent Vanessa one of the three text messages they had agreed upon earlier. The message would inform her that she should accelerate her efforts to get back to her vehicle.

As he stood there and waited on her confirmation of the text, he rationalized that all would be fine. Chances were good that the man he had just put down was the only member of the IT team working this weekend – this was Haiti after all, and Haitians were no different than most other nationalities in that they loved those two final days of the week.

His phone flashed with the message. It was Vanessa: "OMW."

Petit breathed a sigh of relief, opened the exit door and began to make his way to their waiting vehicle.

As he walked a measured pace across the freshly poured concrete parking lot, he reached deep down into the satchel that was still across his shoulders and placed his hand on the grip of the suppressed compact SIG Sauer P365. The pistol was still there, of course.

As he pulled his hand away, it struck Petit that in his profession blank checks were not always about money. For the longest time, this had been an expected, if uncommon, part of the work done by the men and women who served in the CIA or Britain's MI6. But it was something new for Canada and its relatively new foreign intelligence branch in CSIS.

In doing what he had done, it dawned on Petit that he had forced his country to have a long-overdue conversation with itself about just how dangerous the world was, because whether it liked it or not, Canada through his hands, had just become an entirely more serious country.

Chapter 6

Toussaint Louverture International Airport

The room was large enough to hold a pair of battered desks along two of its walls, an equally rough-looking fridge, and a table that held six chairs, all of them different makes, and none of them comfortable.

McCord sat across the table from O'Regan. Michaud was the only other person in the room. O'Regan had directed his 2IC and the Chilean major to wait outside, while McCord had insisted on Michaud's presence.

The Irish general carelessly tossed McCord's tactical pad on the table. "If you're trying to blackmail me, Colonel, you had better find something a touch more stinging than that. My son's unfortunate dalliances are a known commodity where I come from. He has a sickness and it's been dealt with by the courts. I have nothing to hide, and I resent you and your shameful government for daring to mention it under the circumstances. The right people in New York are going to hear about this. Who the hell do you think you people are, anyway?"

McCord reached across the table and picked up the tac pad. His fingers moved quickly as he manipulated the display. He offered it back to O'Regan. "Have another look, sir."

The look on the general's face was one of incredulity. When he refused to take the tablet, McCord turned it back in his direction and started reading. "Brendan O'Regan pled guilty to charges of possession and distribution of child pornography. He was sentenced to two years' probation, three years without access to the internet, and an extended period of therapy. Of Mr. O'Regan, the presiding judge said that the young man had been remorseful for his actions, but made clear that any similar transgressions in the future would be addressed to the fullest extent that the law would allow."

McCord's face was sober. "On the flight down, I looked into... what did you call it? Right, 'dalliance.' What another dalliance might mean for your son. Turns out that Ireland isn't exactly tough on pedophiles."

O'Regan exploded. "He's never touched anyone! He's sick. And so what if he's had another incident? He's my son, but he's his own man. We've done everything we can for him, you son of a bitch. My son's actions will not cow me into turning a blind eye to whatever scheme you're up to. This mission is bigger than my son. It's bigger than my reputation. How far has your country fallen that it would try and use my son's illness to manipulate me? You'll pay for this, Colonel. You. Your unit. Mary mother of God, I'll even go after your prime minister if I can. I'm not without influence."

"You mean your wife is not without influence?" McCord said, his voice nonchalant. "Her family is quite wealthy, it would seem. A shipping magnate father who left her the whole of the company. Not a bad score General."

"This is outrageous! Leave my wife out of this, or so help me you bastard."

McCord placed the tablet down gently on the table and slid it over to O'Regan. "You'll want to have a look at that, sir."

"Colonel Michaud," McCord said, without taking his eyes off the Irish general.

"Yes, sir."

"Did General O'Regan give you an order not to dispatch the rapid reaction force?"

"He did, sir."

"Despite this directive, you took it upon yourself to take your soldiers in an effort to reach the CAF members that were set upon this morning?"

"I did, sir."

"And approximately how much extra time was needed before you could saddle up and move out to reach the soldiers who were still alive on that soccer field after you were told by General O'Regan not to leave the UN compound?

"About five minutes, sir. For instance, it took an extra minute or two to get the Chileans guarding the compound's entrance to open the doors."

"And what time did you arrive at the soccer field after the execution of your soldiers?"

Michaud paused before replying. He wanted to make eye contact with O'Regan, but the man was intently reading whatever information was on McCord's tac pad. "Perhaps five minutes after my men were killed, sir."

McCord placed his elbows on the table and proceeded to crack his knuckles. "General, despite being a coward and having the blood of Canadian soldiers on your hands, my government is prepared to make you an offer that ensures you keep your mouth shut over the next twelve hours as it pertains to my mission."

O'Regan set down the tactical pad. His face was no longer piqued.

"And what do I get for this silence?" said O'Regan.

"Canada doesn't push for a formal investigation into the reasons why our soldiers were murdered earlier today, and we don't tell the authorities in your country that your wife has been indulging your son's penchant for getting off on little boys with images that are not found within the Interpol database. These are fresh images, General, so people – young boys – are, in fact, getting hurt by your son's actions. We give you six months to bury the evidence that implicates your wife, and you have to turn in your son."

"He's sick! Can't you see that? He's not hurting anyone. It's better this way. We can supervise it. We can make sure everyone's safe."

The bottom of McCord's balled fist crashed into the table's wood surface and somewhere in the furniture a loud crack issued. "What part of 'fresh' images did you not understand? Your wife, or the people that she has working for her, are not nearly as clever as they think they are."

"General, you agree to our terms, and you keep your mouth shut, or we bury your wife, her good name, and whatever dreams you have for a career after this disaster of a command. Your son on the other hand, well he's not something my government can turn a blind eye to. He can go straight to hell for all we care."

O'Regan and McCord locked eyes. "Twelve hours?" said the UN commander.

"Much less, if things go my way."

The Irishman gave the Canadian general sitting across from him a baleful stare. "Then you have twelve hours and not a second more."

_____

Communications Security Establishment HQ, Ottawa

With the full run of the Haitian government network, Bahir and his team had become the electronic equivalent of barbarians who had just breached the walls of some poor Roman town. Despite the illegality of everything they had done, they pillaged data with reckless abandon. They had no idea how long it would take the Haitians to figure out their system had been compromised, so every operator in the room was laser-focused on their displays putting their hard-earned skills to full use.

Bahir had organized his team in various sub-units and had even brought in additional operators from the Canadian Forces own cyber-warfare unit to give them extra lift. But once again, he had reserved the juiciest target for himself and the small team that he had brought under his direct command.

In the hour or so they had been ripping through the various files that belonged to the Haitian president's office they had found reams of evidence that suggested the woman was as crooked as a Nigerian internet prince, but nothing found so far suggested she or anyone in her office had any relationship with the Alpha-7s or any foreknowledge of the events that had transpired earlier in the day.

In fact, as Bahir reviewed emails being sent out from the president's office in real-time, he was building the impression that she and her senior staff were as surprised and shocked by the actions of the Alpha-7s as the rest of the world was.

In the corner of his center display, a message flashed: "Need you in Ops Room Bravo ASAP."

"This better be important," he said aloud as he got up from his chair.

"Hey, Kenny."

"Yeah, boss," replied the most senior of his operatives.

"Something's come up. I'll be in Ops Bravo for I don't know how long. Hold the fort and keep plumbing these guys. The moment they shut us down, text me. I'm not sure how long I'll be gone."

"No problems," the man said without taking his eyes off his own bank of displays.

Bahir left their operations room, walked the length of a hallway, turned a corner, and then opened a door with his security pass. The ops room had as many senior folks in it as he had ever seen in one place at the CSE. But it wasn't the executives and military officers who Bahir's eyes focused on. Sitting at the centre of the conference table was Canada's prime minister. He must have looked gobsmacked because his own boss had somehow arrived at his side, grabbed his arm, and guided him to an open seat.

It was as he sat down that he realized everyone in the room was listening to a conversation taking place between two people. He looked at the display at the front of the room and recognized the software that the CSE and the other Five-Eyes nations used to manage the surveillance of various types of telecommunications across the world.

His boss leaned into him and quietly said, "We've tagged Emmanuel Jean's cell phone. That's him talking now."

"The nephew? The guy who took off his mask this morning?"

"Yes, now listen. He's talking to some general."

"I'm telling you, man, now is the time. The old man is gone and we're under new management. I've held up my end of the deal. We killed eleven of the bastards today, and we've got one of them with us. Imagine it. You take power, you announce the death of the old man, and you hand over this soldier bitch to the UN and the world rejoices that there is a new and strong leader of Haiti."

"And what am I supposed to do about you, you idiot? The UN had a drone. Your face is everywhere, you fool."

"And so what? The UN is toothless. Who's going to do anything about it? The Canadians? They're pussies, man. You'll give them back this captain – a little worse for wear, mind you, but once they have her, that will be the end of it. You'll make some type of vague commitment to seek out justice, and life goes on. This is always how it goes in our country, and the Canadians are not the Americans. What can they do? Nothing."

There was a pause of several seconds and then Jean continued.

"General, the international media is an uproar over today's events, our people are upset – they're confused, they're scared. You won't get another opportunity like this. Think of the good you could do. You know she has to go. We need a strong hand to run this country. You are that person, Felix St. Louis."

There was another pause. Finally, the general spoke up. "We'll move at 0100 hours. Have your people do what was agreed to when we met weeks ago, but I don't want to see your face anywhere for the next six months, do you understand? We need to put some distance between today's events and my consolidation of power."

"Six months," said Jean. "So, I'll have to miss out on the celebrations welcoming our new president?"

The general chuckled. "Oh, I'm sure you'll find a way to celebrate. Just make sure you keep a low profile until you hear from me."

"I can keep my head down, and I know exactly how I'm going to bring in this new era of prosperity and leadership for our country. You should see her. Her eyes are stunning. Like jewels looking back into your soul. She's a work of art."

Another chuckle from the general. "See that those celebrations don't get too out of hand. She can't be too damaged when we send her back. If we play this right, Canada still has much to give our country."

Jean scoffed loudly. "I don't tell you how to do your job, Felix. Show me the same courtesy, won't you?"

"Just make sure your people do what they need to tonight. It's critical."

"When I make a promise, General, I keep it. We'll be where we need to be, so you can move at 0100 hours."

The program on the display everyone in the operations room was riveted to changed from green to red.

"St. Louis ended the call," said the Chief for the CSE. "General Hermes, excellent work by your people to get those infiltration units installed. As sick as that conversation was, it's gold for us."

Hermes nodded his head. "I'll be sure to pass along the praise."

The chief's eyes moved onto the prime minister. "Madame Prime Minister, the floor is yours."

"Thank you, Dominique. And I want to echo your words of praise for CANSOFCOM. The infiltration units, the boots on the ground, and a plan, and all of it within hours. It's all work of the highest order, and makes my job a whole lot easier.

"This call was helpful, but before I give my thoughts, I wonder if there's an update from the people who breached the Haitian government's network? What, if anything, does the current president know about what's going on?"

The CSE chief nodded his head in the direction of Bahir. "Bahir here has the lead on that work. What's the latest Ba?"

When he said nothing, Bahir felt his boss give him a sharp kick under the table.

"Ah... right," Bahir stammered. "I can tell you that up until the moment I left my machine five minutes ago, the Haitian government, including the Office of the President, knew nothing about the attack this morning. Everything we've seen or read about today's events on their server is either surprise or anger. Several folks in President Laurent's office mention the Alpha-7s and this Jean fellow specifically, but there's nothing to suggest there was any kind of relationship between the president, her office, and this Alpha-7 outfit. Don't get me wrong, Laurent is as corrupt as the day is long, but as best we can tell, she was clueless about the soccer field attack."

On Bahir finishing his report, all eyes shifted back to the PM. "Then we have enough," she said after a brief pause. "General Hermes, you can move forward with your plan. Based on what I just heard, there's no way I'm leaving Captain Bertrand with these animals any longer than we need to. Get her out of there and we'll deal with the consequences as they come. What else do you need from me?"

"Madame Prime Minister, I have one half of the Canadian Special Operations Regiment ready to lift off in Trenton. I'd like to have them pre-positioned in Turks and Caicos in case things don't go as we hope."

"Approved," said the PM without hesitation.

"Anything else?"

"From the perspective of the military, we're good to go," Hermes said.

The PM's gaze shifted to the other end of the table, where the Minister of Global Affairs and the Director of CSIS were seated. "And what do we do about this general and his brewing coup?"

It was the CSIS director who spoke. "Would it not be helpful if the current president of Haiti somehow received a copy of the conversation we just heard? I suspect CSE could make sure the right people got the file and were prompted to listen to it straight away."

Without so much as a glance in the direction of Bahir or his boss, the chief of Canada's signals intelligence service said, "We can make that happen."

"Okay," said the PM. "Then do it, and do the best job you can to make sure it can't be traced back to us. If we do need to deal with that mess of breaching the Haitian's network, I want it to be several weeks from now. We have enough to deal with for the moment, without having to explain how we broke into another country's protected network, never mind what happened in that server room."

The PM looked around the room with piercing green eyes. "Anything else? Because if there was ever a time to put a concern or suggestion on the table, now is that time."

When it was clear nothing would be offered, she stood up, as did her staff and several of the military officers. "I won't be sleeping tonight, so I'm reachable. And I would appreciate regular updates as best they can be managed. By text is fine. The plan right now is for me to make a statement on the mission and its outcome at 9 am tomorrow. We can shift that if we need to. Good luck, everyone. All of you and especially our people on the ground have done exceptional work today. I'm proud of everyone. Keep it up, and let's bring our people home."

Chapter 7

Toussaint Louverture International Airport

Michaud and McCord walked along the convoy of Canadian Army Mercedes G-Wagons and the eight Piranha-Vs that the Romanians had put on loan to them. Four of the eight infantry fighting vehicles sported a 30mm remotely controlled cannon on their topsides, a level of firepower that would be far in excess of what McCord hoped his commandos would need. The black stenciled UN logos on each vehicle had been painted over in what looked to be slapdash fashion.

Each fighting machine would be driven by one of Michaud's soldiers. They had been in-country going on five months and as a result, his people were much better prepared to navigate the janky and oft-times too narrow streets of Port-au-Prince. The ideal situation would have been for the Romanians to drive the Piranhas, but someone higher up the chain had ruled out that possibility, much to the disappointment of the on-the-ground Euro soldiers.

They stopped at a G-Wagon parked between a pair of the hulking Piranhas. Michaud, kitted up in his full battle armor and sporting a Sig Sauer 226 on his hip, jumped into the driver seat, while McCord settled into the shotgun position to his right. Absent a turret, in the backseat were three JTF-2 commandos. They wore the secretive unit's customized kit, including night-vision goggles atop each of their helmets. Their faces were devoid of emotion. In total, some ninety-three of Canada's most highly trained soldiers would assault the Alpha-7 compound, with a hundred of Michaud's Vandoos being held in reserve.

Beside him, McCord said, "Open channel, Task Force Gamma."

Less than a second later, Michaud's earbud came alive, and he could hear the colonel speaking in his ear. With no delay between McCord's voice in the earbud and the man seated beside him, he decided he could manage the two points of communication.

Canada's regular army regiments hadn't yet been issued the Battle Area Management system or BAM as yet, so he, and those of his soldiers who would drive the commandos, had received a crash course on how the near-AI-facilitated comms system worked. Of the full BAM kit, they had only received the earbuds, so they could only listen to McCord and his soldiers as they communicated or issued orders. If Michaud and his drivers needed to communicate amongst themselves, they would do it via the tried-and-true radios in each of the vehicles. He checked his watch. It was just after 0100 hours.

"Alright, everyone, you know the plan," said McCord. "Lead vehicle, you're a go for Waypoint Gamma. Move."

Instantly, Michaud heard the rumble of the convoy elevate as drivers shifted the transmission of their vehicles into drive and began to move forward.

If all went according to plan, they would hit Waypoint Gamma in twelve minutes and then the Alpha-7 compound in another twenty. As the eight-wheeled Piranha in front of him began to move, he shifted their G-Wagon into drive and in a low voice said, "Hold on, Vee. We're coming for you."

Operation Caribbean Payback was officially underway.

––––

Alpha-7 Compound

Bertrand saw the blow coming. When it struck, an explosion of stars laced her vision. She was again seated on the stained mattress in her windowless room. The new, self-anointed leader of the Alpha-7s stood above her, his legs straddling her hips. He wore a smile that showed off his ill-kept teeth. Breathing hard, she could smell his breath. It was rank. As he stepped back from her, she spat a mouthful of blood and saliva onto the floor at the man's feet.

He smiled at her and wagged his index finger at her. "I like that. You've got spirit inside you. Not like most of the women I have. For all the poverty in my country, too many of the girls I like are on too many drugs. They're numb and too compliant. But not you. No, you're very much alive. And your eyes. Oh, your eyes."

The man inhaled sharply and stared at her. "This is going to be like magic. Rough. Hard. Magic."

As his hand went to his belt buckle, there was a loud knock at the door.

"Fuck off!" the gang leader roared. "I'm busy."

"Boss, it's urgent," the muffled voice said from behind the door. "Ricard has a guy on the phone who says he needs to speak with you. He says it's an emergency. He's got an accent and his French is terrible. We think he might be with the UN. He'll only talk with you."

Jean stared down at Bertrand. As a sneer took over his hideous face, he issued a guttural scream. Stepping back, he moved to the door and ripped it open with a savage jerk.

"Give me that," Jean said, pointing at the phone one of the two men was holding out.

Putting the phone to his ear, he barked, "What?"

Bertrand strained to listen, but could only make out the garbled sounds of a phone too far away. As the gang leader listened to the person on the other end, the sneer of anger on his face transitioned into what she thought was a look of concern.

After two minutes of listening, the gang leader said, "I know who you are. I don't know why you're calling, but don't think this conversation means anything. I owe you nothing."

But then the line must have gone dead because the gangster let the cell drop from his ear.

Jean tossed the cell back to the man that had given it to him and turned his eyes onto Bertrand. He spoke with a calm voice. "It looks like your government is coming to get you, Captain. An unexpected and stupid move on their part. More of your countrymen are going to have to die."

He turned to face the two men in the doorway and thumbed in the direction of Bertrand. "Get her up. Paul, I want you to have her ready to move in five minutes. Have three vehicles ready to go at the north entrance. I'll meet you there."

"Sure thing, boss," the leaner of the two men said.

The gang leader turned his attention to the other man who had a wicked-looking scar running down the right side of his face. "In about ten minutes, Canadian soldiers are going to try and take this compound to take back this new prize of ours. They can't have her. Gather the men and you kill as many of those devils as you can. Kill them all for all I care. They don't know we know they're coming, so you'll have the advantage. Make the most of it."

Jean took a step toward the man and with his right hand, drove his index finger hard into his lieutenant's chest. "And no surrender, Louis. This is our country and our city. You make them pay for their arrogance, and you get paid extra for every additional piece-of-shit soldier you kill today. Are you clear on what needs to be done, my dangerous friend?"

The sadistic smile that crawled onto the thug's face was accented by his puckered scar. "Perfectly clear, boss."

———

"Bap, we have movement of several vehicles at the compound," said Cole. "Make that three SUVs. They're rolling from the front of the compound to the back. I have movement in several other places as well. Jesus, the place is like a pissed-off beehive."

"They know we're coming," said Baptiste. "Get the drone down to two thousand feet. As best we can, I want to be able to see individual faces. If they're gonna move her, I want to know which vehicle she's in."

"Copy that. Repositioning now."

Baptiste activated his BAM. "Open Channel to Razor Actual, priority call Alpha-Hotel."

After a wait of a few seconds, Baptiste said, "Sir, we have a burst of activity at the compound. Personnel and vehicles are on the move. Lots of hostiles carrying weapons. I think it's a safe bet they know you're coming."

Baptiste paused to listen and then replied, "Copy that, Razor. We'll work to make that happen. Badger Actual out."

Baptiste picked up the radio handset on his lap and toggled it. "Drapeau, get us to the north side of the compound, but not too close. We'll follow you. It looks like we have three vehicles getting ready to make a run for it. Keep your lights off."

"Copy that. I know just the spot. Rolling now," said Drapeau over the radio.

Twenty meters ahead of them, he saw the CSIS officer's beat-up white 4Runner start to move. Baptiste put his own vehicle into drive and followed.

"McCord said they're moving ahead with the mission. If they move Bertrand, we are to follow, and if we can interdict, that's our call. You still ready with those three packages?"

Seated beside him, Cole was manipulating what looked like a video game controller and appeared to be pouring all of his concentration in the direction of an oversized tactical pad on his lap.

Without taking his eyes off the tac pad, the JTF-2 mission specialist said, "The packages are ready to go, boss. Razor only needs to say the word and shit goes boom. And our bird is where it needs to be. I'm gonna be hard-pressed to see faces, but if someone is cuffed, hooded, or being carried, I'll be able to make it out."

"Aces," said Baptiste. "Cause if we get the chance, we're gonna take down these bastards hard."

————

General Felix St. Louis of the recently re-constituted Haitian National Army was several vehicles back from the head of the convoy. As Haitian coups went, it was not a bad showing. In the short time he had been given, he had gathered some three hundred soldiers and a similar number of police. Military officers and police supervisors loyal to his cause were now spreading across the city to seize key buildings, including Radio Haiti, where, upon his successful taking of the National Palace, his soldiers would announce to the country and the rest of the world that he had taken power in an entirely justified and bloodless revolution for the people.

He would not make the same mistakes as the leaders of the infamous '91 coup. Under no circumstances would Haiti's current president be permitted to leave the country. There would be no negotiations with the Americans, the French, or the United Nations.

Just like those men who had come before her, Haiti's current president was a ravenous leech who had been draining the country's finances dry from the very moment she took office. Once in control, he would reveal her graft and other crimes and it would be announced that she would be imprisoned. And while she languished in the shit and heat of one of Haiti's jails, her supporters would be purged. Many had been complicit in President Laurent's crimes and like her, they would pay for what they had done.

He heard the squelch of the radio of one of the two officers sitting in the front seats. At that same moment, he felt the vehicle coming to a stop. Looking ahead, he could see the lead vehicles of the convoy had halted their advance.

A voice came over the radio. "We have six vehicles lined up across the road. There are perhaps two dozen soldiers and policemen amongst the vehicles, all of them armed. It doesn't look like they're going to let us pass."

"Bullshit," said St. Louis as he looked to the large man sitting beside him. "Phillipe, come with me. It must be François' men who've messed up their orders. That man is useless."

As he stepped onto the pavement, Phillipe Auguste, the third most senior man in Haiti's National Police force, followed him out of the SUV and together they walked to the front of the convoy.

They had been traveling down Rue Oswald Durand. Another kilometer down the thoroughfare was the National Palace. Indeed, as he looked down the stretch of road, there were six police vehicles blocking their route. They were lined up bumper to bumper, with one end of the blockade flush against the outer wall of Sylvio Cator Stadium. As he took in the scene, he caught movement along the stadium's roof that overlooked his convoy.

As his mind assessed the scene, a voice boomed in the night air over the rumble of close-by vehicles. "General Felix St. Louis, this is Director-General Henri Constant of the Haitian National Police. I have a warrant for your arrest. Please come forward with your hands above your head. You are under arrest." The amplified voice was coming from a loudspeaker from somewhere beyond the vehicles.

"He can't be serious?" St. Louis said to the tall policeman standing beside him. "How the hell did they find out? No, don't answer that. It doesn't matter. There's only a few dozen of them and there's hundreds of us. There was always a chance this was going to get ugly, Phillipe. Call up the men, and let's get this over with. We have a schedule to keep."

As he turned and started to walk back to his SUV, he heard his main collaborator and right hand begin to shout out orders to the men around them. "I want Unit Fifteen up here on the double, and I want two machine guns set up and ready to hit the stadium rooftop. There are at least twenty men up there. Move, you lazy pissants!"

"General St. Louis, this is your final warning. Come out now or we open fire," said the man on the loudspeaker, his voice echoing off the walls of the stadium and buildings around them.

On reaching his SUV, he pivoted back to the blockade. He could hear several engines revving behind him as soldiers and policemen began to move forward. They might no longer have surprise he thought, but there was no doubting his men's determination. They were as sick of the president and her corruption as he was. He could see it on their faces as they hustled past him with their weapons. They would not be denied and neither would he. Haiti needed new leadership. His leadership.

To his left and in the direction of the city's port, he first saw and then heard the first of the explosions.

As the skyline to the north lit up, a concussive boom rolled over him. Less than a kilometer away, the detonation was both deep and foreboding. As he took in the blooming spectacle of light another explosion went off behind him – this one in the west of the city. Turning, he saw a ball of fire glowing in the distance. Further away than the first blast, this explosion's boom took several seconds to reach him.

"What in Christ's own name is going on?" he said loudly as he put his hand on the door handle of his vehicle. As he swung it open, a third explosion rocked the early morning. This one was to the east. It was the biggest of the three by far. The light from whatever was combusting surpassed the energy from the first two blasts. St. Louis both heard and felt the explosion as it reached his position. All around him, buildings shook, and the walls of the country's largest stadium reverberated.

He looked back in the direction of the blockade only to see Auguste was running back to him. As the big policeman's legs pumped, he was pointing frantically to the north. The normally unflappable man had a rare look of concern on his face.

St. Louis turned in the direction Auguste had been pointing and took in the dark sky that lay above Port-au-Prince Bay. He immediately picked up two specks on the horizon. The half-moon was directly behind them, so whatever was there was plain to see. Planes? Were they planes? As the two objects began to take shape, he picked up glints of moonlight dashing off what must have been the glass of the jets' canopies.

"Mother of God!" he yelled.

As the words left his mouth, the two fighter jets screamed over their position. Well under an altitude of five hundred feet, the roar of their engines was deafening. Soldiers everywhere dived for cover and several of them were yelling, "The Americans, the Americans. The Americans are coming!"

He ignored the hysterics and kept his eyes on the two planes. They had banked slightly on hitting the city's waterfront and were now over the southeast quadrant of the capital. The sound of their engines still ringing in his ears, he watched intently as the two planes produced a stream of bright red flares and then suddenly jackknifed high into the night sky.

He took his eyes off the jets and focused on the slowly descending, brilliant red orbs. He closed his eyes and concentrated for a second. There was a nibbling at the back of his mind. It was a sensation that life experience had told him to pay close attention to. He waited, letting his mind do its work. The flares were coming down on a part of the city he knew better than most. That was important, he thought. And then it struck him like a freight train. The Alpha-7s. There was no doubt about it – the flares were coming down right on top of that bastard Jean. "They can't be serious," he yelled over the chaos of noise that surrounded him. "Who the hell do they think they are?"

And then he was struck by something else. He would use this to his advantage. The explosions, the jets, and soon enough, the killing. All of it would shake the nerves of the men on the blockade and whoever else got in their way.

He looked at Auguste who was now standing in front of him. The large man was breathing heavily but appeared to have his wits about him. "Who are you talking about, Felix? Who are they? What's going on?"

"Phillipe, the jets are not for us. Nor the explosions. They are here for that thug Jean. He went too far today. Much too far. The Canadians are going to try and take back their officer. Come, my big friend. We must rally the men. Opportunity still stands before us on this night. Now is the time for us to be bold!"

Chapter 8

Port-au-Prince

"We have people coming out of the north side of the compound," Cole advised calmly.

The tac pad was leaned on the console between the two seats. The high-end infrared camera easily picked up the various individuals spilling out of a set of doors on the north side of the main building. While several of them formed a perimeter around the three SUVs, others began to climb into the vehicles.

"Got her!" said Baptiste triumphantly. Two men were coming down the stairs and between them was a third person.

"I see them," said Cole, and a moment later, the drone's camera expertly zeroed in on the descending trio.

"They've got her blindfolded," the younger JTF-2 operator said. "They're putting her in the second vehicle."

"Alright, let's see which direction they take her. If they know their business, they'll go in the direction opposite of where McCord is coming from."

"Incoming priority call from Razor Actual," said the calm and synthesized voice of Baptiste's BAM.

"Approved."

"Badger, we are two minutes out from the compound, you are a go on fireworks. I say again, execute on the fireworks."

"Copy that, Razor," said Baptiste. "I can confirm with a high probability that our package has left the building. She's entered one of three vehicles. We've got our eyes on the convoy. They are leaving the compound on the opposite side from your approach. Advise next steps."

"Badger, execute on the fireworks. The package could be a ruse. We'll take and clear the compound but will send part of the task group in your direction to assist with the takedown of the convoy. Observe and take it down as the opportunity presents. We have Blackjack on standby if needed."

"Copy that, Razor," said Baptiste. "Fireworks are imminent, and we'll stay on the convoy. Will keep you updated. Badger Actual out."

Baptiste looked at Cole. "Light 'em up, son. McCord will be on the compound in a minute."

Cole smiled, held up his hand, and made a series of quick taps on his BAM wrist unit.

Seconds later, Baptiste heard the first explosion, a small fuel depot located at the port. The second explosion, far in the west of the city, was smaller but still managed to make one hell of a sound. The third and final detonation was the largest by far. Less than a kilometer away, and with a secondary fuel source twice as big as the fuel depot at the port, Baptiste heard and felt the third explosion boom and rock the immediate area.

At street level, in and amongst the houses and shanties of this part of the capital, he couldn't see the blast directly. Instead, as the structures around them rattled violently, the street laid out before their SUV danced with an army of excited shadows as light from the nearby explosion fought a pitched battle with the early morning darkness.

"Nice," exclaimed Cole. "That's what you get with five pounds of C-4 and three thousand liters of diesel."

To his credit, in setting off the blasts the younger soldier never took his eyes off the tac pad and the black-and-white infrared image of the three SUVs leaving the Alpha-7 compound. The smaller, gated north-side entrance of the stronghold had been opened for them and as soon as they hit the roadway, all three vehicles turned left and accelerated like scared cats.

"Looks like they're headed our way, boss," Cole advised.

Baptiste brought a hand-held radio to his mouth and toggled the unit. "Ady, the package has left the building. Follow us. We're going to get ahead of them and see if we can't execute a takedown."

"Copy that. We're right behind you, Actual," replied the Montreal cop.

Baptiste put their own 4Runner into drive and punched the gas. As they sped forward, the street was beginning to fill with people who had come out of their homes to see what the hell was going on. As he expertly dodged and weaved and made ample use of the vehicle's horn, he heard the roar of two F-35s fly over their position at a near-supersonic speed. Again, buildings rumbled and shook. On the streets, a few of the locals looked up and pointed at the retreating jets, while many others scampered back into their homes allowing Baptiste to pick up speed. As he drove, out of the corner of his eye he caught the blazing red flares that the two RCAF fighters had unloaded on top of the Alpha-7s' compound. One hell of a calling card, he thought.

"Cole, my man, I don't know this part of town. You're gonna have to navigate. Can you get me out in front of them?" As Baptiste asked the question, he jerked the steering wheel wildly to avoid colliding with a gigantic woman who, despite her size, had somehow quickly waddled into the street with her eyes looking skyward.

"Keep moving on this road for another klick and then take a right and then the next left." Cole could have been reading out this week's grocery list, the commando's voice was so nonplussed. "Looks like they're encountering the same problem we are. Locals are everywhere."

He slowed down their vehicle and honked his horn ferociously at a throng of people that had bunged up the street. He leaned his head out of the window and in Haitian-accented French, bellowed for the spectators to get out of the way. In between his yells and the sound of the horn, he caught the faint pop of automatic gunfire and several small explosions. JTF-2 had reached the Alpha-7s. Let the main event begin.

––––––

Alpha-7 Compound

The first Piranha-V hit the steel gate at the southern end of the compound doing forty kilometers an hour. At seventy-three thousand pounds, the eight-wheeled Infantry Fighting Vehicle drove through the barrier as if it were paper mache. It was quickly followed by three more of the Romanian armored machines.

On breaching the outer gate, the four armored vehicles turned on their high beams and flooded the façade of the largest building with light. In total, the compound was perhaps two acres in size. In pairs, the four IFVs quickly traversed several dozen meters of well-manicured lawn, sending plumes of torn soil and grass high into the air. It was at fifty meters out from the main villa that dozens of automatic weapons opened up on the approaching Canadians.

As rounds began to impact their thick steel hulls, two of the four machines slammed on their brakes while projecting their ample lights on the compound's central villa. The two remaining IFVs roared past them in the direction of the main building's grand, staired entrance.

The lead Piranha quickly rolled to the start of the forty-degree staircase and without pause, its five-foot high wheels quickly churned up the stairs and crashed into the front entrance of the building at twenty kilometers an hour. With a crack of sound that momentarily surpassed that of the ongoing gunfire, the whole of the armored vehicle disappeared inside the building.

Theecondd IFV, not far behind the first, negotiated the stairs more slowly, and instead of recklessly following the first Piranha, it expertly edged its nose into the jagged maw that was now the main entrance of the building.

As gunfire poured down on the exposed rear end of the second fighting machine, commandos in the first Piranha emerged from their vehicle's topside hatches and its rear-end ramp and began to engage with those Alpha-7s that had hastily run from their windowed positions deeper inside the compound. As the first wave of panicked gangsters ran into the airy foyer with guns blazing, the waiting JTF-2 commandos efficiently cut men down in screaming and bloody heaps.

On the grounds of the compound, Canadian G-Wagons poured through the main entrance. Those of the up-armored SUVs that had turrets, had soldiers in them operating pintle-mounted C-6 general purpose machine guns. Each of these guns belted out short bursts of 7.62mm rounds at the various positions in the villa where enemy fire had been flagged. Those G-Wagons without turrets raced to the destroyed entrance and from each of the four-by-fours, commandos exited their vehicles and, under fire, ran up the colossal staircase to enter the building.

Inside, twenty-odd special operators from the two breaching Piranhas were now outside their vehicles, had stacked up in classic house-clearing formations and had already started the process of moving into the building.

The scene in the foyer was as close as you could get to having a living, breathing bull inside an actual china shop. Debris from the destroyed entrance lay strewn everywhere. On the ceiling, a huge, still-functioning chandelier was unmoored and hanging cockeyed. Underneath the third left tire of the lead Piranha, an unlucky Alpha-7 lay dead, his upper body crushed and smeared across a once-spotless Italian marble floor.

With dust hanging in the air and the boom of suppression grenades echoing from within the building, JTF-2's second-in-command, Lt. Colonel Marc Fortin, watched and listened to his men carry out their work like the professionals they were. Word over the BAM was his men were now on to the second floor. Good, he thought. They were making excellent time. A warning – and that's what it had been – hadn't made much of a difference for the Alpha-7s. Street thugs were no match for highly trained and fast-moving soldiers – not with only ten minutes of lead time. If anything, the advance notice had meant more of them had had to die.

As more of his commandos moved past him, the near-AI voice in his earbud said, "Call from Razor Five."

"Approved," said Fortin.

Captain Still's voice jumped into his earbud. "Sir, we've cleared the basement. There weren't that many rooms. We think we've found the location where they were holding Bertrand. It's empty."

"Copy that, Razor Five. I'll let Actual know. Finish your business, and then get your ass back here. Razor One out."

"Call Razor Actual, priority call, authorization Delta-Whiskey."

A second later, he heard McCord's voice. "Marc, what's the story?"

"Looks like Bap was right, sir. It doesn't look like she's here. We'll have the rest of the place cleared in the next ten or so, but she's not where we thought she'd be."

"Okay, great work. Finish up, get whatever intel you can, and then get out of there. Baptiste has eyes on the convoy, and he's working up a takedown as we speak. We're not far behind him. McCord out."

———

"Take the next right," Cole said, as unconcerned as ever.

Baptiste yanked on the steering wheel hard and as he negotiated the corner of the narrow street, the engine of the twenty-year-old 4Runner strained. "Just hold a bit longer, you son of a bitch."

"We're ahead of them," Cole said. "The street they're on is filled with people. They're moving at a crawl. There's an intersection coming up. That might be our best chance, Bap."

"How far is McCord?"

"About five minutes out."

"What's the intersection look like? Any civies?"

"Right now it's clear."

"How's the sky?" asked Baptiste.

Cole popped his head out of the window. "Crystal clear."

"You're sure they put her in the middle vehicle?" Baptiste asked again for what might have been the fifth time.

"One hundred percent, boss."

"Tag the lead SUV."

Hearing the order, Cole's fingers quickly worked over the tactical pad issuing the required orders to the drone that had been observing the Alpha-7 convoy. Seconds later, Cole said, "Lead vehicle is tagged."

Baptiste activated his BAM. "Open channel for Blackjack, authorization Hotel-Uniform."

"Blackjack, this is Badger Actual. Confirm you've received our tag."

"Badger Actual, I can confirm the tag. I see lots of civies on the ground."

"Copy that, Blackjack. The target is moving west and will break away from the civies in moments. I need you to immobilize the target at the intersection about eight hundred meters west of their current position? Can you make that happen?"

"Copy that, Badger. A piece of cake. We have the right package and as long as you keep the target lit and it's clear of civies, we'll take it off the board. Setting up our approach now. Stay at least fifty meters back from the intersection. Blackjack out."

———

Blindfolded, Bertrand couldn't see anything, but she could hear every word being said and didn't need a degree in psychology to glean that the man sitting beside her was not happy.

"Get these people out of the way. Shoot them if you have to!" the Alpha-7's new leader yelled.

Whoever was driving laid into the horn once again. And then, for the first time, she heard automatic gunfire come from within the vehicle. The ear-splitting noise came from whoever was in the front passenger seat. A man cursed and screamed for people to get out of the way. Seconds later, she heard another burst of gunfire which was quickly followed by a collection of howls and ferocious curses from outside the vehicle.

"Finally!" she heard the gang leader say. Suddenly, the vehicle lurched forward, its engine straining as they began to pick up speed.

"Almost there, boss," someone said. "Past this intersection and a few more turns."

"I know where we're going," Jean snapped. "What? Do you think I'm a fool? Just get us there, Manny, and keep your mouth shut."

She felt the vehicle slow down. The intersection, she surmised.

"C'mon," yelled Jean. "What are you slowing down for? There's no one on the road, for Christ's sake."

As the driver's foot hit the accelerator, Bertrand was thrown into the back of her seat, but just as quickly, her ears were assaulted by a massive boom and, through her blindfold, she was able to take in a flash of light. The SUV or whatever they were driving in slammed on its brakes and in the process violently tossed her into the seat in front of her.

As one, the men inside the vehicle howled obscenities. As she heard the panic in their voices climb, the acrid chemicals of whatever had just blown up began to assault her sense of smell.

"Get us out of here!" Jean bellowed.

Once again, the vehicle lurched forward, but before it could gain any kind of momentum, Bertrand heard someone scream, "Jesus! To the left. Look out!"

As she heard the screech of tires, she instinctively lifted her feet off the floor and braced herself against the seat in front of her. The other vehicle slammed into the front end of the Alpha-7 SUV at speed. Not buckled into her seat and with her hands bound behind her, the physics of the collision violently jacked her body to the left forcing the side of her face to slam into the window that she had been seated beside. Instantly, she saw stars and felt a sharp, stabbing pain as glass from the shattered window sliced into her scalp.

Ignoring the pain, Bertrand forced herself to take in a series of deep breaths and concentrate on those senses available to her. A man who wasn't Jean said in a deep voice, "They're armed. Move out of the way!" As she felt a jostling of people in the back seat, she could sense the person that had been sitting beside her had moved. Her adrenaline on overdrive, Bertrand forced herself to move her bum off the seat, and lowered her profile so that she was squatting on the vehicle's floor. No sooner had she done so than nearby gunfire ripped through glass and metal, and someone inside the vehicle grunted in pain.

"We need to get out of here! Paul and his men should be right behind us. Grab her! We can use her as a shield if we need to," said the now-familiar voice of Jean. The gangster's voice had a desperate edge to it.

Bertrand felt a pair of large hands grip the shoulders of her fatigues and drag her backward. Whoever had grabbed her, their strength was formidable. Despite her efforts to resist, the man easily tore her from the position she had wedged herself into on the SUV's floor. For an instant, she felt her body fly through the air as she left the vehicle on a horizontal plane. As gravity asserted itself and her beaten body slammed into the asphalt, Bertrand let out a sharp yelp of pain.

Again, the same strong pair of hands grabbed her and hauled her to her feet. Swaying but managing to stand on her own, she again heard the voice of the Alpha-7 leader. Filled with equal parts fear and outrage, the gangster screamed an order for someone to kill her. Though her eyes were still covered with the blood-soaked blindfold, Bertrand squeezed her eyes tight, uttered a quick prayer, and waited for the bullet that would end her life.

———

The GBU-35 Urban Use Bomb hit the lead SUV dead center on the far side of the intersection. The explosion of the one-hundred-pound laser-guided bomb shook their SUV and lit up the night sky.

"Go, go, go!" Baptiste barked into the handset he was holding at his mouth. In front of them, Drapeau gunned his 4Runner and after a twenty-meter sprint, the CSIS agent slammed the four-thousand-pound vehicle into the front right wheel well of the black SUV that held Bertrand.

Already outside their vehicles, Baptiste, Cole, and Ady moved toward the intersection like a pack of wolves on the prowl. Baptiste and Cole moved in the direction of Drapeau's now-smoking SUV, while the Montreal drug unit officer peeled off and took up position behind a utility pole, focusing the sights of his C8 carbine on the third vehicle of the convoy that had pulled up thirty meters short of the collision. Its engine running, no one had yet left the relative security of the SUV's steel frame.

As they approached the rear end of the CSIS officer's 4Runner, Baptiste's right hand came off his weapon and knifed in the direction of the right side of the SUV that carried Bertrand. Silently, Cole broke off and made a beeline to the driver's door.

Baptiste moved along the left side of the crashed vehicles and took in the sight of Drapeau gingerly extricating himself from the driver's seat of his 4Runner. Both feet on the ground, the intelligence agent flashed him the okay sign and fell in behind him, his Sig Sauer now drawn.

With the CSIS man now on his six, Baptiste continued forward to the crumpled front end of the Alpha-7 vehicle. Despite the orange light from the bombed-out vehicle on the far side of the intersection dancing across the SUV's windshield, he had a clear view into the vehicle. The man in the front passenger seat was laid out on the dash and was unmoving but the driver of the SUV was conscious and fiddling with something on his lap. Suddenly, the man's left hand stabbed forward with a handgun pointed in the direction of Cole, but before he could get off a shot, Baptiste heard a burst of suppressed gunfire. The man's upper body jolted as several bullets ripped through steel and glass and into flesh.

The rear passenger door on Baptiste's side of the SUV quickly swung open. The head of a gigantic man poked above the tinted window. At a range of ten feet, Baptiste placed the reticle of his own Fabrique Nationale P-90 at the center of the door's window, but just as he was about to pull the trigger, there was movement, and the legs and feet of a second person joined the giant behind the open door.

Less than a second later, the huge thug shuffled around, ducked out of sight, and then a green-clad body flew out of the vehicle onto the rough asphalt. The door of the SUV still open, the brute of a man stepped toward the figure on the ground, exposing his entire frame, and as though he was grabbing a bag of potatoes from the market, he reached down and easily hauled the prone and moaning body to its feet.

"Kill the bitch!" yelled the voice of the man who was still behind the open door of the SUV. As the giant reached for a handgun tucked into the front of his belt, Baptiste fired two quick rounds into the man's exposed flank. As each of the bullets entered him, the henchman flinched and turned his massive body in the direction of Baptiste. With a grimace of pain on his face, the man bellowed incoherently and tried to level his weapon in Baptiste's direction. Without hesitation, Baptiste sent a round into the man's forehead, collapsing the giant to the ground in a massive heap.

With Drapeau now beside him, they advanced on the blindfolded soldier standing in front of them. Halfway to the person who must have been Bertrand, he heard a long exchange of gunfire on the other side of the SUV.

Hearing the screech of tires, his eyes darted down the street toward the third and last vehicle of the convoy. It was reversing into a crowd of people that had chosen to remain on the street despite the orchestra of violence underway. Hundreds of people dodged and moved, allowing their numbers to swallow up the retreating vehicle. Baptiste took in the crowd. While some of them screamed or spat in the direction of the retreating Alpha-7, most faces were turned in their direction. They didn't have much time.

As he reached the still-open door, he stepped around it and leveled his weapon into the backseat. Inside was a pudgy, sweat-drenched man who had pressed himself against the far side of the vehicle, his hand on the door latch. The man, Emanuel Jean, gave Baptiste a hateful look, opened the door, and hurled himself onto the street, starting to move in the direction of the surging crowd. Cole, still on the other side of the SUV, was on the fleeing man in an instant. The muscle-carved commando and former Bishop's University football player moved like human lightning and drove the butt of his rifle into the back of the man's skull, instantly dropping the gangster to the pavement.

Baptiste and Cole locked eyes through the length of the SUV. "Get him ready to move. He's coming with us."

"Copy that," Cole said.

He heard a woman's voice and pivoted to see Drapeau helping Bertrand remove her blindfold. Though blood was streaming down her face in bright red rivulets, he could see that other parts of her face were swollen and covered in ugly purple bruises. As Drapeau cut the restraints off her hands, he again glanced in the direction of the crowd. In the few seconds he took to assess the approaching threat, Baptiste couldn't see any weapons, but it was also the case that the locals were far from happy. If they rushed them, they wouldn't have a chance.

Someone in the crowd yelled, "They're Americans! Fuck you, America! Go home." Another person further back in the advancing throng threw a good-sized rock in his direction, but their aim was off. More debris followed.

He turned back to Bertrand. "Are you good, Captain?"

Her face shone with determination. "A hundred percent."

"Good, then let's move."

Drapeau led the way and soon they were joined by Cole and Ady. The two men, both built like brick shithouses, were easily dragging the Alpha-7 leader between them. As they made their way to their remaining still-running 4Runner, Baptiste urged them forward while keeping an eye on the advancing locals. The mass of humanity had enveloped the collided SUVs and, in the process, would have gained access to whatever weapons the Alpha-7 henchmen had on them. Somewhere at the front of the crowd, he saw the flash of a knife blade.

As he walked backward at the rear of their small group, he activated his BAM. "Open a channel for Blackjack."

"Channel Open," advised a synthesized female voice.

"Blackjack, this is Badger Actual. We've secured the package, but we've got a growing crowd of unhappy locals breathing down our necks. Any chance you can do a fly-by?"

"Roger that, Badger. Will be on your position in two mikes. Blackjack out."

As they reached their vehicle, Baptiste said, "Ady, you drive. Captain, in the middle seat in the back. Cole, get in the cargo area with that piece of shit. Drap, you're with me."

With the CSIS agent at his side, he turned to the hundreds of faces quickly moving in their direction. While some were curious or were sporting smiles, most faces had an ugly look to them. This country's people had suffered tremendously for three straight generations and much of this misery had been caused by the international system that Canada worked so hard to uphold. That they were Canadians and not Americans would make little to no difference to the angry folks who were now arrayed before them.

And rightly so. As it pertained to the hemisphere's poorest country, Canada was no patron saint. Haiti was not in the top ten of Canada's foreign aid program and Canada's immigration system had long been a well-traveled highway for tens of thousands of Haiti's best and brightest to abandon their country. As he thought about it and sidestepped another flying rock, perhaps it wasn't a bad thing that this crowd thought they were Americans. At least the Yanks carried a big goddamned stick – maybe that's why they hadn't taken a run at them.

He heard the double-tap of the 4Runner's horn and turned his head in the direction of the CSIS officer. "Slowly, my friend. If we run, this gets ugly. Play it cool."

As he took a step backward toward the SUV, to his right he saw a too-thin man with several missing teeth step to the front of the crowd. He was holding a handgun. He held it in the air and fired off several rounds. Around the agitator, angry men with desperate looks on their faces both flinched and bayed. As the rest of the crowd built up a collective roar, the armed man pointed the pistol at Baptiste.

"Shit!" Baptiste said aloud as he trained his rifle on the crazed-looking man. Suddenly, the crowd in front of Baptiste was lit up by a wall of bright light. Behind him, he heard the roar of diesel engines, and a pair of Canadian Army G-Wagons stormed into the space between him and the crowd. As both vehicles blared their horns, the called-for RCAF F-35 shrieked across the sky. Flying just above the level of the rooftops, the power of the jet's engines rattled buildings and deafened ears. Under the sudden onslaught of sights and sounds, the mass of people took a disjointed step backward.

He looked at Drapeau and over the cacophony, barked the order to move. Together, they turned and raced to the waiting 4Runner. The Montreal policeman had positioned the SUV such that it was facing away from the human wave. As Baptiste reached the door, he pulled it open and launched himself into the seat. He slammed into Bertrand who had braced her hands on the seats in front of her. On the other side of Bertrand, Drapeau too jumped into his seat.

"Move, Ady!" Baptiste ordered. The on-loan army reservist popped the horn twice signaling to the commandos they were on the move. A second later, the 4Runner's tires screeched, launching them toward safety.

Chapter 9

Toussaint Louverture International Airport

"Baptiste, grab Bertrand from the medic. I need to talk to both of you pronto," said a striding McCord.

"Copy that, sir," Baptiste said.

He gave Cole, Ady, and Drapeau each a quick look and said, "Hang tight, boys. Back in a few."

As he began walking toward the small medic station they had set up in the hangar, he heard Ady call, "Boss, when you're talking to the higher-ups, see if they're serving beer on the plane. I need myself a drink, active duty or not."

Without looking back, Baptiste waved his hand in the air to acknowledge the army reservist's request.

As he approached the medic station, he and Bertrand locked eyes. She was sitting on a cot and had an IV line in her arm. Seeing that he was taking in the line, she said, "It's a precaution. Apparently, I was low on fluids. What's up?"

"McCord wants both of us. I don't know what he wants. He's out back. Can you part with the get-up?" he said, pointing to the drip in her arm.

Without hesitation, Bertrand detached the catheter and got to her feet. "I'm good. Let's go."

A minute later they were standing in front of the special operations commander. Soldiers were everywhere keeping an eye on the immediate area, but none were within listening distance of the tall colonel. The man had his usual no-nonsense look.

"Listen, there's no easy way to put this," he said abruptly. "To get us out of here without starting our own little war, I may have to give Jean back to these bastards."

On hearing the words, Baptiste quickly unloaded. "That's bullshit, Gord. Fucking bullshit and you know it. You know what this guy did."

McCord's face softened as Baptiste's words struck him. "Lenny, I know it's shit, and you know me. If there was another way, I'd do it, but I need to get us out of here in one piece and I need to think about the soldiers who will stay with the UN. The word is coming straight from the PM – Laurent is coming with us, and she'll be given refugee status in Canada among other things. Jean is the only bargaining chip I have. I don't like it any more than you do, but it's what we've got."

McCord turned his eyes onto Bertrand. "Listen, Veronique, I know what this man has done to you and it's tearing me up inside that I might have to let him go. It's not what any of us want.

"And for what it's worth, the PM is not happy about the situation either and she wanted me to tell you directly that this Jean bastard isn't off the hook. It's just that justice for you and your men is going to have to wait."

McCord paused and then said, "Before I head out there and speak with the newest crook that will run this country, I wanted you to know. I owe you that much and I'm sorry. You deserve better, but I know you know the score."

Bertrand, who had been standing with her hands on her hips, moved to cross them over her chest. Her jaw tightened visibly. Standing at her side, Baptiste could tell she was doing her best to hold back tears. He was beyond furious that they were doing this to her.

"We should have popped that fucker when we had the chance," Baptiste said.

"It's okay, Lenny," Bertrand said in a firm voice. "The colonel's right. We need to get out of here without any more fighting and I need to bury my men. I need to see their families. I need to see my family."

She looked at McCord and said, "Tell me what the PM said about Jean. What did she say exactly? If we're going to do this, I need to know what she said."

McCord hesitated. Baptiste could see that he was weighing whether or not he should disclose what the country's leader had said to a junior officer, even one that had experienced what Bertrand had. "Screw it," the colonel said. "This is for your ears only, Captain. Lenny, not a goddamned word to anyone, understand?"

"It dies with me," said the commando.

"Alright, as you know there's an election coming up and the PM's chances don't look great, so early this morning, she had a conversation with the leader of the opposition.

"I don't follow politics closely - who's that again?" asked Bertrand.

"Bob MacDonald. He's from Saskatchewan and from everything I've heard about the man, he's solid. In any event, the PM and Mac-Donald came to an agreement. Regardless of who's in office, the Haitians are to be given a year to sort out Jean. If they don't do what needs to be done to our satisfaction, we'll take care of it ourselves, whatever that means."

"It means there's a good chance I'm coming back to Haiti," said Baptiste dismissively. "I know this cursed place as well as anyone, Gord, and they ain't gonna do anything to that piece of filth. This country is a den of thieves. You don't need more proof than the past twenty-four hours."

Bertrand's arms uncrossed and her hands went back to her hips. Absent of any moisture in her eyes, she looked at McCord with a hard glare. "If we're coming back, I have to be part of it. Some way, somehow. Promise me Colonel. The CAF and the country owe me that much."

McCord didn't hesitate. He thrust out his hand in the direction of Bertrand and their hands locked. "Indeed, we owe you that much, at the very least. You've got my promise, Captain. If we have to come back, you're in."

National Palace, Port-au-Prince

"We've rounded up the last of the resisters, sir. Those who would talk to us advised that Laurent and several of her cabinet ministers were headed in the direction of the airport."

The tall policeman who was St. Louis' right hand was sweat-soaked and had a horrendous smell about him. The fighting to take the National Palace had been intense. Though outnumbered four-to-one, the defenders of Haiti's president had been ready and had fought well from hidden and solidified positions. Dozens of his men had died, but they had found their mettle and pushed on to victory. In the end, the defenders had run out of ammunition and were forced to surrender.

"Excellent work, Phillipe. We've done it, my big friend. The president and her cronies are on the run. No doubt she's hoping someone with the UN will fly her out of the country. Under no circumstances can we let her leave. I won't repeat the mistakes of '91. She does not leave. Do you hear me? She has raped our country, and she will account for her actions here in Haiti. The international community can go to hell," St. Louis said as he took note of the first signs of the rising sun.

"Yes, general," said the towering man.

"Secure the palace and then gather as many men as you think reasonable, and let us head to the airport. We'll block the runway and force the UN to hand her over. Today will only be a great day for our country if we can make Madame Laurent pay for her crimes."

As he took in St. Louis' words, the man who would soon command the country's national police force gave a well-executed salute and said, "Yes, sir."

Pivoting away from St. Louis, Auguste lumbered purposefully in the direction of a gaggle of army officers and policemen and began to bark out a series of orders.

The sight brought a smile to his face. With the help of competent men like Auguste and with his own willingness to lead and make hard choices, St. Louis would make this country right again. He knew it just as he knew his coup would be successful. He could smell destiny in the air, he thought. The smell of burning vehicles and petrol, the smell of blood and sweat that lingered on the men around him. It was both potent and heady. He just needed to hold things together a bit longer and he would have his prize.

————

Toussaint Louverture International Airport

They were in the hangar where McCord and his commados had unloaded only a few hours before. Outside on the tarmac were a pair of grey RCAF CC-150s, their engines running. JTF-2 operators and his own soldiers from the Royal 22nd Regiment surrounded the two planes on foot and in several G-Wagons. The Romanian Piranhas were further afield either watching the main entrance leading into the airport or facing off against the dozen or so police and army vehicles now occupying the runway.

When their convoy with Captain Bertrand had arrived, it had been dark, but now as Michaud looked out onto the tarmac of Haiti's national airport, dawn had begun to reveal itself. It had been a long night and it stood to be an even longer day.

He turned away from the crumbling sea of asphalt and the idling transport planes and locked his eyes onto McCord. The special forces officer had been speaking to someone via his BAM for the past five minutes.

They had been advised of the St. Louis coup attempt in the middle of the assault on the Alpha-7 compound. At the time, McCord had taken the news in stride. "More chaos means more room for us to do our thing, Mich. We'll make it work for us," had been his sage-like response at the time.

McCord's less laissez-faire take on the coup had changed markedly when he had been advised Haiti's deposed president and a large part of her political entourage had been waiting for them inside the hangar with General O'Regan at their side.

After issuing a few choice curses and giving orders to further secure that part of the airport they were occupying, McCord had brief and separate conversations first with the Irish general and then Haiti's freshly deposed leader. He watched the JTF-2 commander listen intently to both parties. The square-jawed man had offered little to the president or the UN commander other than to pronounce that he would need to check in with Ottawa to get direction about how to proceed.

As they strode away from Haiti's former president, McCord pronounced, "Well, Mich, you can't make this shit up. The world is a crazy place, eh?"

"And few are crazier than this country. So, what's the plan, sir?" Michaud asked.

"As I understand it, the leader of the coup – this General St. Louis fellow – is waiting to talk to me out on the runway. Care to undertake some international diplomacy?"

"I've come along this far, so why the hell not."

"Indeed, you have, my friend. And my apologies now for all the grief you'll have to endure once my men and I leave this land of confusion. Another coup is just what the poor people of this country need. Jesus, what a fucking mess."

As they began to walk in the direction of a huddle of G-Wagons, McCord thumbed back toward the hangar they had just left. "Do me a favor. As I think about it, grab that Irish bastard. Best he's part of what happens next."

"Sure thing, Gord. And if he says he doesn't want to come?"

"Oh, he'll come, Mich. He thinks we're tits up and that my outfit isn't getting off this island. That Irish son of a bitch wouldn't miss that for the world. My guess is that he'll insist on coming."

———

General St. Louis, Haiti's president-in-waiting, stood in front of a dozen army and police vehicles lined across the mid-point of the Toussaint Louverture International Airport's only runway.

"Here they come. Finally. Another ten minutes, and I would have started to melt. They had better have her in the back of one of those vehicles."

"Sir, those APCs with the guns on top. If they start shooting at us, we can't protect you out here," Auguste said.

St. Louis waved a dismissive hand in the direction of the approaching military vehicles. "Pay them no mind, Phillipe - no one is going to shoot anyone. Whoever is leading these soldiers is many things, but he's not stupid."

The two eight-wheeled armored vehicles leading the convoy peeled off allowing four of the Canadian-owned SUVs to continue in their direction. Rolling left and right, the huge fighting machines took up positions that would allow them to quickly flank St. Louis and his soldiers. The remote-controlled machine guns atop both of the growling vehicles were not pointed at his men but looked menacing all the same.

The four SUVs stopped twenty meters in front of him. On top of two of the vehicles, soldiers stood in turrets, their shoulders braced against the stocks of heavy machine guns. These, too, were pointed away from him and his men, but the faces of the soldiers operating the weapons gave him every reason to believe that could change in an instant.

As the doors of the SUVs opened, several beefy men wearing body armor and carrying a variety of weapons, spilled out and loped forward to corral a threesome of soldiers who were not wearing helmets or body armor. The way the security detail prowled forward and surrounded their charges reminded St. Louis of time he had spent in France where he had briefly done some training with that country's special forces. These were special operators, of that he was sure.

As the delegation arrived, he turned his full attention to the men who were at the center of the protective bubble. Interestingly, each man wore a different colored beret – one tan, one green, and one blue. The blue, of course, was that of the UN. The Irishman, he knew on sight. The other two men he did not recognize, but he guessed they were Canadian and weren't with the UN mission.

He stepped forward to meet them. "Gentlemen, thank you for coming, though I must say your tardiness stands to impact our discussions. I am a patient man, but I have limits. I trust President Laurent is in one of those armored beasts you've brought with you?"

The square-jawed man with the tan beret took a step forward. "General St. Louis, I'm Colonel Gordon McCord and I have the authority to represent the Canadian government in this matter."

St. Louis looked at O'Regan. "I thought this was a UN mission? I doubt your masters in New York have given authority to the colonel here to speak for anyone. Is the Security Council even aware of Canada's egregious breach of my country's sovereignty? If they don't, they will soon, and you'll have a lot to account for, General."

"The UN, my command, and I myself had no advance knowledge of the Canadian's plans. I'm as outraged as you are, General. Colonel McCord seems to be under the illusion that he and his government can act with impunity. Well, I see things quite differently, as you can imagine. But all that said, I've agreed to be here to bear witness to whatever agreement you might come to."

The Canadian colonel offered no reaction to O'Regan's scornful tone or words. St. Louis' eyes zeroed in on the flagpole of a man in the tan beret. "So, Colonel, it would appear you are operating unilaterally. I trust you understand there is only one way you, your men, and your planes will be using this runway?"

The Canadian's face was like granite. He said nothing. Instead, he slowly lowered his hand into one of his pants pockets and pulled out a smartphone. He took a step in the direction of St. Louis. "Sir, I need you and General O'Regan to listen to a recording. Would you mind coming a bit closer?

"Colonel McCord, my demand is simple and my patience is all but drained. Whatever games you want to play, you can save it. Bring me the president now, or this whole affair goes in a direction none of us wants. As I said, I'm a patient man, but it has been a long night, and there's been too much death already."

The tall Canadian handed his phone to the third, and to this point silent, officer to his right. He then turned to O'Regan on his left and roughly grabbed the Irishman and all but dragged the smaller man toward the coup leader. O'Regan growled in protest but nonetheless allowed himself to be marched forward. As the two men reached St. Louis' position, the silent soldier held out McCord's phone and proceeded to manipulate the display.

Before St. Louis could put his voice to the outrage now frothing within him, he heard the pathetic voice of that fool Jean and then he heard his own voice, as confident-sounding as ever. He recognized the conversation instantly.

St. Louis almost physically cringed when he heard the other man use his full name. As the dialogue played out, his heart rate began to accelerate. Just how the hell did they get that recording?

Offense, he thought. Go on the offense, just as he had been doing all night long. This could be managed if he played his cards right. He didn't have nearly as strong a hand as he might have had only five minutes ago, but the situation could be salvaged.

St. Louis' upper lip curled into a snarl. "How dare you insult my intelligence? There are people in my own country who can deep fake a conversation, never mind the technology that you might have access to in yours, Colonel. This is below your government, and it changes nothing. This is your last chance. Bring me President Laurent or else you give me no choice."

McCord raised his hand in the air and made a fist. Over the man's shoulder, St. Louis saw the ramp of one of the armored fighting vehicles begin to lower. Seconds later, he saw a pudgy man with a black hood on his head emerge, led by two bulky soldiers. The two commandos frog-marched their captive forward, stopped ten meters from his position, and in a quick flourish one of the soldiers' gloved hands yanked the hood from the mystery man's face.

St. Louis fixed his gaze on the blinking eyes of the newly minted Alpha-7 leader. He wouldn't have believed it if it wasn't for his own eyes, but there he was. The vicious little gargoyle was standing in front of him as plain as day. This was not good.

"General St. Louis, with the recording I have just played you, with the confession of Mr. Jean and with other evidence my government has collected, I am advising you now in no uncertain terms that should you fail to permit my men and the current president of Haiti to leave your country, that Canada, with all the diplomatic weight it can muster, will secure a warrant for your arrest and will see you prosecuted internationally for your complicity in the murder of eleven Canadian soldiers and the egregious mistreatment of one of my fellow officers."

The Canadian colonel paused for a moment and said, "Sir, your name can be added to the long list of war criminals that continue to waste away in some shitty European prison, or we can make a deal."

After a long moment of staring daggers at Jean, St. Louis turned his eyes back on the colonel wearing the tan beret. The bastard was as stone-faced as ever. The man would have been a nightmare to play in poker. "And what type of deal are you offering, Colonel McCord?"

The Canadian officer did not hesitate with his reply. "Now and at no point in the future, will my government use the information we have collected to prosecute you or to stymie your governance of Haiti. This would include your time as leader and beyond. Effectively, on this matter, we're offering you immunity."

"And what do I give you in return, and how is it that I know your government will keep its word?"

"You let my two planes leave and on those two planes will be the current president and Mr. Jean. Ms. Laurent will take up residence in my country with a pension courtesy of the Canadian taxpayer on the condition she remains out of Haitian politics."

McCord paused for a moment, and then thumbed in the direction of the bound gangster. "Your Alpha-7 friend also comes with us, but there's no sweetheart deal waiting for him. Instead, he gets tried for the murder of the aforementioned soldiers and for the other crimes I believe you are aware of." As he said the words, McCord's face transitioned from impassive to thunderous.

For a too-long moment, St. Louis said nothing. His head was spinning as he tried desperately to work through various scenarios that could play out depending on his answer. In the end, he played the cards in the manner that had got him to this point. "Your proposal – if that's what you can call it, is outrageous. My men and I will die before we let that corrupt bitch leave this country. If you knew what she's done, you'd hang her yourself. She needs to face Haitian justice."

He then pointed in the direction of Jean. The man's round face had a pleading look upon it. "And that piece of shit. That recording you played is fraudulent, but there is no doubt in my mind that this criminal played a central role in the death of your soldiers. He too will face Haitian justice."

He turned to face the Canadian officer. "Turn both of them over to me, Colonel, and I let you leave. It is that or more blood on your hands."

The Canadian officer's jaw tightened. "There are four hundred more soldiers one hour away from your country, General. And in Canada, there are another thousand sitting on a tarmac just like this one – all of them paratroopers who will land anywhere they please. Each and every one of them will make your life and whatever government you hope to set up a pipe dream. And you've seen our jets. A full squadron will be moved into the region within the day. One way or another, my planes are going to leave this airport. I spoke with our prime minister directly not fifteen minutes ago. She's one determined lady, General, and she doesn't give one speck of shit if we have to fight our way off this island or not. That I'm standing here before you should be proof enough of that."

St. Louis smiled. "Colonel, you threaten me and my country all you like. It may be true what you say – that you can have your soldiers here and that you could leave by force, but what damage would that do your own country? You are out on a limb, my friend. If you fight me and my people, that limb might snap and when you fall into the jungle below, you have no idea what awaits you. Haiti can be a dark and savage place. You know this. Is your prime minister prepared to play such a danger-ous game?"

For the first time during their conversation, the Canadian's face softened, if only slightly. He then exhaled deeply. "Listen, I want to make this work. There's been enough dying already, to be sure, and under your leadership, your country gets a fresh start. That's no small thing, General. You can trust the word of my government and run this country for however long you can hold onto it. We'll make sure Ms. Laurent lives a quiet life. We know about her proclivities, we know about her secret bank accounts, we know how much she cares about her nieces and nephew and the education they are getting at various elite schools across the world. We have quite a bit of leverage on her. She'll come to understand what's on the line if she hasn't already. Let her come with us. As one military man to another, I promise she'll live a quiet life and that you'll have a free hand – at least from us."

"A quiet and happy life with funds she's taken from the Haitian people. How is that justice?"

"You're a politician now, General. Politicians have to make com-promises all the time. Madame Laurent will be the first of many in the coming days I suspect."

St. Louis' eyes left the Canadians and took in the day's burgeoning sun over the man's shoulder. The morning's vista had turned out to be muted. Not everything would be perfect on this day and the Canadian was right - he would have to make compromises. Many of them.

"You've not mentioned Jean, Colonel. Perhaps we can achieve a compromise on him. As you've asked me to trust you with our jackal of a president, I think it's only fair that you reciprocate with the gangster. To be perfectly candid with you, the man knows too much and despite the evidence of today, your country is soft. Your government might keep its mouth shut but Jean will not. I know this man – he is a sieve and worse, he is weak. With the press in your country, you know what will happen. He'll be given interviews and it will all spill out. Considering all that has happened, I don't think that's in either of our country's interests. Give me Jean, and I will let you leave with that devil of a woman, despite my hatred for her."

"Then we have a deal, General, but with one condition."

"Oh, and what would that be?" St. Louis said, with the hint of a growl in his tone.

"I'll leave the Alpha-7 with you, but we're not done with him. One way or another, we'll see justice done. In five weeks or five years, we'll come for him if he doesn't pay a price we feel is right."

The Haitian officer bristled. "The right price? Who are you that you can stand before me, in my country, and dictate how justice will be served?"

St. Louis took a step closer to McCord. "How about this, my new friend. I'll accept your threat of infringing upon my country's sovereignty yet again, but it will be with my own condition."

When McCord remained stone-faced, the Haitian continued. "There are many of my countrymen in your country are there not, Colonel? And is it not a small and wicked world that we live in? Yes, you can send regiments of soldiers into my country, but your government is not the only one who can make threats. So my own condition is that you pass along a message to that woman you want to set to your country's tit. Tell her and the political masters that control you that she lives at my pleasure and that if she cannot abide by our agreement, we will do to her as you would do to Jean. Will you pass along that little quid pro quo, Colonel?"

McCord's reply was immediate. "With all due respect, General, I won't pass along the message."

The Haitian took another step forward. The two men were now less than a foot apart. Though shorter than McCord by some measure, the wiry Haitian held himself as though he were the larger of the two. "Oh, and why is that, Colonel? Tell me why you won't afford me the same courtesy that you're dictating to me?"

"Because my country is not your country. We do not allow, nor will we tolerate the savagery that is too common in the world that you live in. You do what you want here, General. Make Haiti better or make it worse, I don't particularly care, but what you will not do is infect my country with whatever justice you might want to see done to Madame Laurent."

"Ah, and there it is." One of the Haitian's hands had come up slowly, an accusatory finger jutting out toward the center of McCord's chest. "Western hypocrisy on full display. You get to lay down a boldface ultimatum to me, but I'm given no such luxury. Do as I say, not as I do. So very colonial and white of you, Colonel. I wonder if I shouldn't reconsider this deal of ours?"

As it had been for most of their conversation, the Canadian's face remained implacable. From what St. Louis knew of them, the Canadians were a sensitive bunch when it came to things like race. Well, tough, he thought in that moment. The Western world's record in his country had been appalling and if he needed to play the race card to level the playing field with the man standing in front of him, he was prepared to do that. There was too much at stake, and it wasn't as if the accusation was untrue.

When McCord finally spoke, it was in the same matter-of-fact tone that he had used throughout the negotiation. "Here's the bottom line, General. I get to dictate things because my country is stronger than yours and because it is right, and it is just. If you have a slice of honour in your body, and I think you do, you know this is true.

"So here's what I'm prepared to do - we'll keep our end of the bargain regarding Madame Laurent, but if we feel the need to return to this part of the world to set things straight with that piece of garbage who helped you come to power, we'll do so because we can but only because you made us. Don't make us, General. Because I promise with the full weight of my government, if we need to come back to this sorry country of yours, it will not end well for you. You accept the reality that is this deal or you don't. The choice is yours."

St. Louis offered no reply but instead took a step around the JTF-2 commander and walked in the direction of the Alpha-7 gangster. With the Haitian general a dozen feet out from the Canadian's captive, the two soldiers flanking Jean looked to McCord.

"Captain Still and Sergeant Wright, step away from the prisoner if you please," McCord yelled across the distance.

Their weapons at the ready, the two commandos moved several steps back from Jean.

Arriving at the gang leader, St. Louis stopped to the left of the man and pivoted to lock eyes with McCord. The man's face now had a grim look to it. In a quick movement, St. Louis' right hand unholstered the silver revolver that had been on his hip and leveled it at the side of Jean's head.

"Wait, no... Felix!" the Alpha-7 leader cried.

Without a word, Haiti's newest president pulled the trigger.

As the bullet from the pistol punched into the gangster's skull, the exploded contents of the man's brain scattered across the tarmac. The moment Jean's lifeless body struck the asphalt with a sickening thump, St. Louis casually lowered his gun back into its holster. His eyes were now back on McCord. They were dark and more penetrating than they had been only moments before.

"I accept the terms of your deal," St. Louis said in a raised voice that easily carried the distance between the two men. "Take your soldiers and that witch from my country and never come back to Haiti. And when you arrive back in your country, make sure that you honor your end of the bargain as seriously as I have. Because now you know exactly who you're dealing with, and how very serious I can be. Do we have an understanding, Colonel?"

"We do, General," said McCord. "A crystal-clear understanding."

———

As Michaud, McCord and the Irish UN mission commander turned away from St. Louis and his entourage and made their way back to their respective vehicles, McCord said, "General, would you ride back with Colonel Michaud and I? We have something to discuss."

"No, Colonel. After what I just witnessed, I don't want to be seen within five hundred miles of you. As I made clear at the beginning of your little horse-trading session with the man you just anointed as Haiti's new president, I was here as an observer only. Despite your heroic efforts to destroy the impartiality of the UN's current mission in this country, events are such that we may be able to avoid most of the shit you've managed to spread over the past twelve hours or so. Of the many things that came out of that travesty of a conversation you just had, I can't help but think St. Louis knows that the UN had nothing to do with today's debacle."

The exceedingly fit commander of Canada's tier-one military force stopped walking and, after a couple of steps, so did O'Regan. The reedy man turned to face McCord. "We're done here. We have our deal. I honored it and if I'm to believe the conversation you just had with the new president of Haiti, you're a man of your word. So get off my island and take all of your men with you. Those dead and those still alive."

McCord once again produced his phone. "Are you sure you don't want to do this in a more private location, General? I can't foresee what might happen once I play you the following."

O'Regan shot the Canadian a baleful look. "Another recording. You're just chock-full of them, aren't you? Well, you know as well as I, whatever you think you might have will be worthless at the UN. Deep fakes are all too common in this day and age. St. Louis wasn't wrong about that, the fool."

McCord hit play on the smartphone and despite the noise around them, the sound of the recorded conversation carried the distance between the two men. Michaud listened to the dialogue between a man speaking in heavily accented French and a man he knew to be Emmanuel Jean.

When the conversation finished, McCord had dropped the poker face he'd struggling to wear for the past hour. His face and stance, the way his fists tightened at his sides – all of it suggested the man was two strides away from an explosion of violence.

"That conversation took place exactly twelve minutes before my men hit the front gates of the Alpha-7 compound. Tell me, General, how is it that at exactly 1:19 this morning you found a disposable phone and got your hands on Emmanuel Jean's number? Remarkable, don't you think?"

For a moment, O'Regan's face was that of a stunned deer on a midnight highway. The man sputtered and said, "Even if that's not a deep fake, you can't prove that's my voice. That wasn't me. I'll deny it. You have nothing."

"It doesn't matter," McCord said, jaw tight and his voice almost at a yell. "You've forfeited our deal, you Irish prick. You put my men's lives at risk, you worked against the interests of my country, and most importantly, you worked against what is moral and right. We're gonna find out what type of relationship you had with that sick bastard Jean, and when we do, we're gonna pull every political lever we have access to and we're gonna call in every favor that's due to us, so that we can bury you, your wife, and that pedophilic kid of yours. Whatever life you thought was waiting for you after this mission is over. You're done, you hear me? And this isn't me who's making this threat, General. All of Canada is gonna come down on you like a goddamned freight train."

Across the few feet they were separated on the tarmac O'Regan offered McCord a resentful stare, but the Irishman said nothing. Rather, he turned and strode in the direction of the vehicle he had arrived in.

As the departing man in the blue beret got out of hearing range, Michaud issued forth a low whistle and said, "Well, that should make the next few weeks pretty interesting. I'm assuming that my soldiers and I will stay with the mission?"

McCord continued to stare at the back of the departing UN commander. As O'Regan got into his designated G-Wagon, the JTF-2 CO turned to Michaud. "As we speak, Global Affairs is putting on a full-court press to have that duplicitous bastard removed as commander, among other things. Until that happens, keep a close eye on your soldiers, your orders, and keep flying the flag. If folks back home do their jobs well, few people will know the full extent of what we just pulled off. It will be lost in the noise of this country's most recent political shit-show."

"It's too bad about this country," offered Michaud. "It's people have this incredible combination of resilience and hope. If they were just given a chance, I bet they could make a real go of it, but based on what I just witnessed, it looks like Haiti's run of bad luck will continue."

As they reached their vehicle, McCord stopped and took in the other officer. His face was one of resignation. "We don't do this country and countries like it any favors by taking its best and brightest. We, and by we, I mean Canada, are like a vampire sucking the heart and soul out of these people one immigrant at a time. And on top of it, we leave people like this St. Louis fellow in charge while simultaneously bailing out the most recent corrupt jackass. Just think of the good a person like Baptiste could have done in this place."

"Maybe. Or perhaps the conditions of the country wouldn't have shaped Baptiste into the man he is today. I imagine the Warrant Officer could have been one hell of a gangster," said Michaud.

"Or he could have been the cop who finally cleaned this place up. We'll never know, Mich. And that's just how it goes. Thank goodness we live in the country we do."

———

Months Later, Montreal

As she walked out of the lecture hall, she thought about the professor's proposal. He had offered to take her out for coffee a second time and like the first time, he had been a gentleman about it.

As she left the building and walked into the warm air of yet another spectacular fall day in Montreal, she once again marveled at the number of trees that littered the city. It was such a contrast to home, where the vast majority of trees and forests of Haiti had long ago been felled for one terrible reason or another.

And they didn't have 'fall' back home. Not like here. Not like this. The season was at its height and the yellows and oranges of the foliage contrasted magically with the powder blue of the October sky. It was a picture and it filled her with a happiness that escaped her on most days.

She had declined the professor, but as she had departed the classroom, he had forewarned her he would ask one more time in the coming weeks. But only one more time and then he would let it go, lest she think he was being too forward. It was nice being pursued. Particularly by someone who had some idea of how it was done. The rest of the men in this city could learn a thing or two from her sociology professor.

And why shouldn't she go on a date with the man? Yes, she was his student, but it's not like she was eighteen. She would be twenty-six next week. She was a woman in every sense of the word and when you looked at the matter rationally, if she continued to deny the opportunity of a relationship with the man, she was being a prude.

Based on her short time here in Quebec, she could attest that prudishness was something that was in short supply. The men were as forward as any back home, and by all accounts the women welcomed it. She could do the same. There was nothing stopping her except that promise she had received. But that was eight months ago. Surely in that amount of time, he could have made contact with her? It's not like she was hiding or didn't want to be found. But he hadn't reached out and from where things stood at the moment, she was beginning to feel like quite the fool.

In a sea of interested men, here she was waiting for her prince charming to walk into her life and sweep her off her feet, like some bad romance novel. For pity's sake, the man had been a spy and she had been a secretary. A well placed one mind you, but a secretary nevertheless. No doubt he had a bevy of women he could call on. All she ever was to him was an 'asset'. No, she thought to herself, the next time the professor asks to go for a coffee, she would say yes and she would see where that led. Jesus, a date didn't mean she had to marry the man, she told herself.

Her stroll from campus terminated at the bus stop that would bring her home to her too-small apartment where she no doubt find her mother trying her best to entertain her daughter. She had wanted to find something larger and nicer, but the stipend the Canadian government was providing only went so far in a place like Montreal. At least for this month, they had enough food. The foodbank around the corner from her place had made sure to increase their regular allotment of items after she told them they had almost run out of food last month. It was her daughter. How could something so small be so ravenous?

"Excuse me miss?"

The words came from behind her and jerked her out of her domestic musings. The man who had asked the question was close. Now that he had made his presence known, she could feel him standing behind her. He wasn't too close like that creep she had warned off a few weeks back, but he also wasn't that universal two-meter distance that everyone was expected to observe when dealing with people outside of their immediate social bubble. And then there was his voice. Her memory was tickled by it.

Slowly, she turned and saw him. Tall, handsome, broad-shouldered. The smile on his face was both wonderful and kind.

"Good to see you, Van," he said. "I wonder if you might have time for a coffee. I know a place just around the corner. They have this neighborhood's best pastries."

She couldn't help herself - her eyes began to well. The man moved forward confidently and took her hand. As his skin made contact with her own, it felt good. It felt better than good. It was as though in that moment their molecules had begun to merge. As she looked into his eyes, she finally managed to say, "You came."

"I made a promise."

"You did."

As a tear left her eye, his hand rose to her face and gently wiped at the pearl of moisture.

"Sorry, I don't mean to cry. I'm being stupid."

The man continued to smile and after a moment repeated his invitation, "Coffee?"

Vanessa laughed and said, "Yes, yes, let's have coffee. I've been waiting forever for this to happen. And maybe one of those pastries. I'm starving."

"Then let us go. I suspect you and I have many things to discuss," the man said while offering her the crook of his arm.

"We do. Like where have you been all of this time? I've been so worried about you. No one would tell me anything. It's as if you never existed."

As they began to walk down the street under an auburn canopy of fall-ripe trees, he said after a time, "I'm glad you waited. I had left the country not long after you, but my work had kept me busy. A lot had happened, so there were lots of questions."

The way he said the word 'question' brought a look of concern to Vanessa's face. "Is everything alright?"

"All is well. The right people made the right decisions and now I get to be here with you. As promised. I'm only sorry it's taken so long."

"Don't be sorry. You're here now and that's all that matters."

They continued to walk and somewhere in the distance, they heard a siren followed by the revving of a determined engine.

"Do you remember the other promise you made me?"

"I do."

"Then what is your real name?"

The man gently stopped their progress. Unlinking their arms, he turned to face her. Slowly, so as not to alarm her in any way, he reached out with his large strong hand to take in her delicate one.

As their hands clasped, the man said, "My name is Petit, Samuel Petit. But you can call me Sam. And it is my pleasure to meet you, Vanessa. A pleasure indeed."

The End.

Afterword

Dear Reader,

First, a huge thank you for reading *Caribbean Payback*.

It is my first novella and was written as a reader magnet for my newsletter and as a lead-in to my first full-length novel *Take Whiteman*, *the CANZUK at War* series, Book 1.

I really enjoyed writing *Caribbean Payback* - the story came to me easily and I really liked its characters. I hope to use one or more of them in the sequel to *Take Whiteman*, which I hope will be published in early 2023.

One thing that is critical to authors is reviews. This is perhaps more true for new authors. If you purchased *Caribbean Payback,* I would love for you to leave a review on Amazon or Goodreads. All feedback is greatly appreciated. Honest review included.

In addition to leaving a review, you are welcome to write to me directly to give me your feedback about *Caribbean Payback*. I would love to hear from you and will most certainly get back to you. I can be reached at: raf@raflannagan.ca

Again, thanks for reading my first novella.

R.A. Flannagan

Copyright

Cover design by Ares Jun: aresjun@gmail.com

Special thanks to my editor: Stephen England

Special thanks to my beta readers: Bob Flannagan, Karen Flannagan, and Matt Dunn.

Other Works

Take Whiteman, **Book 1 of the** *CANZUK at War* **series**
<u>**Pre-Order Today!**</u>[1]

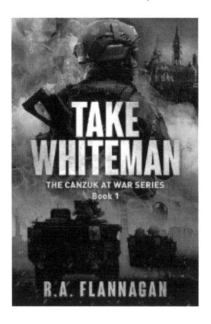

CANZUK: An alliance formed of Canada, Australia, New Zealand and the United Kingdom

————————-

The United States is into the third year of a terrible civil war. Once great American cities are now nuclear wastelands.

As the world watches the former United States tear itself apart, Canada and the CANZUK alliance can standby no longer. Their freedom on the line.

---
1. http://raflannagan.ca/

A Canadian paratrooper, a British tanker and an Australian commando lead their countries into the former United States and a war that will shape the rest of the world.

In Canada, an untested deputy prime minister is confronted by an unthinkable home-grown plot and shadowy international forces who do not want her country to succeed.

Through the eyes of frontline soldiers and pilots, intelligence officers and political leaders, Canada and her allies must overcome insurmountable odds to secure not only its freedom, but the freedom of democratic states across the world.

Take Whiteman is a first of its kind a techno-military thriller written for Canadians but it is a story that will resonate with anyone who keeps a close eye on world events.

Fans of Clancy (*Red Storm Rising*), Bond (*Red Phoenix, Vortex*), Lunnon-Wood (*Long Reach*) or Greaney (*Red Metal*) will enjoy this action-packed, politically savvy near-future novel.